MAPPING EDEN

For Jonathan Klijler,

With warm

regards,

Carol Japhe

June 2021

Mapping Eden

Carol Japha

CROTON ROAD BOOKS

Copyright © 2021 by Carol Japha

Cover map: Nicolaes Visscher, Map of the Holy Land or the "Earthly Paradise," 1657 (detail)
Author photograph by Katherine Weiland
Cover design and layout by Johanna Miele Graphic Design

Published by Croton Road Books, P.O. Box 4852, Greenwich, CT 06831

ISBN: 978-0-578-83852-6

Manufactured in the United States of America

For Kate

CONTENTS

Prologue

We had a photograph on our piano, in the sunroom in the front of our apartment on the North Side of Chicago. The sunroom had little black-and-white mosaic tiles on the floor, like in the bathroom, and windows all around.

The piano took up the entire sunroom. It said "Rudd Ibach und Sohnen" above the keyboard. They said my mother used to play.

I didn't like to look at that photograph. It's in my desk drawer now, face down, in its metal frame with the flip-stand on the back.

It shows a sweet, half-turned, slightly out-of-focus face.

She's almost smiling in the picture, but she wasn't smiling at me.

She left. She vanished. She didn't say goodbye.

I didn't want to be reminded.

I didn't like to go into the sunroom, with the grand piano and the photograph and the dust motes dancing in the shafts of light.

The dust motes, feathery, loft and drift. In the darkness the dust motes vanish, you cannot see them.

You don't think about them when you can't see them. Maybe they don't exist. Like the music that used to come out of the piano. I don't mean the sheet music, which was stuffed inside the piano bench, under the flip-top seat. Later, someone gave it away.

I couldn't remember the music. Had I heard it?

What I had known I could no longer be sure of. What had felt real now seemed a dream.

She was gone. Had she ever been?

People talked in front of me but not to me. They whispered behind their palms. They halted their words mid-sentence.

Best not to speak about it, pretend it wasn't happening.

I never said a word. Of course, not a word was said to me.

My father was a doctor, surely he knew all about it.

My father knew things that other people didn't, carried around a storehouse of knowledge, secrets in his head. These weren't the kinds of secrets you told your friend or your friend told you—things you weren't supposed to tell. They were things other people could know, might know, but generally didn't—didn't know the way he did.

My father taught me to orient a chart by the points on a compass. He introduced me to the earth—what it looks like and how it got that way. He revealed marvels of climate and land. He could list the conquests of Charlemagne and name the highest European peaks. He recalled the distance from Berlin where he grew up to Freiburg where he studied, and what time the trains departed and how long was the journey.

My father talked of the distant past as if it were yesterday. He remembered the birthdays of the aunts and uncles and cousins on the family tree he spread out on the living-room rug, and liked to speak their names as if I knew them. He kept the letters they sent from the far-flung places they had fled to, written in handwriting you don't see any more, certainly not now, handwriting of another language and continent and age. He kept the stamps, taught my brother how to soak them off the envelopes and put them into albums.

But he didn't like our questions, mine and my brother's. Especially mine. Robbie was older. I learned to stop asking them.

No one said out loud why my mother was gone and all the other mothers were there. It could have been a secret like the things my father knew, things out of books. But it seemed like the other kind of secret, the kind you were punished for telling.

I
Geography

❦ 1 ❧

We were already different—our apartment filled with Old World furniture, dim landscape prints, china that never was served. The only foreigners on our Chicago street.

My father in his formal, threadbare jacket, with his fine manners and esoteric knowledge.

My mother . . . She slips in and out of view. I try to get her, and the long-ago past, in focus.

We had come from other places, which I never saw or could barely remember.

We had brought our furniture with us, dark pieces too ornate for a Chicago apartment, and set them down in the living room holding down the edges of the frayed Oriental rug. In the marble-topped buffet with Adam and Eve carved on the doors were stacked the gold-trimmed dishes that weren't, in our day, taken out even for Passover, because we didn't celebrate Passover. In the rosewood bureau with curved-front drawers that stuck opening and closing were linens too large for any table we owned or any gathering of the few people we knew or got to know, stiff damask watermarked with flowers or trimmed with crochet lace.

In one corner of the living room my father's desk and bookcase made an L, the desk against the wall with a tiny window above and the bookcase meeting it. Opposite this

L stood his armchair, where he settled in the evening after supper to read the newspaper and his medical texts and journals.

The armchair faced into the room across from the couch. When company came, they might sit on this chair, though we never did. It was my father's.

His desk was piled high with papers and journals. You couldn't see the surface.

In the top center drawer my father kept the long, thin scissors he used to clip articles from *The New York Times*, which he filed inside book covers, on shelves, in desk drawers, wherever they fit, according to his own scheme of classification: temperature records and ball scores, the lives of the monarchs, the deaths of people he remembered from another time. We were allowed to open that one drawer, where he kept the scissors and stamps, three-cent stamps they were then, in case we needed to mail a letter. We were allowed to use the scissors, but only to cut paper. They were paper scissors.

We had our furniture from England and Germany before that and new things that mostly were cheap and already wearing, though they were much newer. We had books, rows of Gibbon and Churchill, bursting with clippings, Edith Hamilton and *The Story of Mathematics* and the *Brockhaus Encyclopedia*, my father's prized possession, published in Berlin c. 1910, the year he was born.

My father had books in strange German lettering and medical books with frightening pictures and scientific books filled with equations and histories of thin, dense pages. Maps were in some of them—the *Brockhaus* and the *Historische Schul-Atlas* and the *Holy Land Atlas,* where you could see Abraham traveling from Ur to the land of Canaan, Joseph going down into Egypt, and the Israelites following their long, slow, zigzagging way back. You could locate the territories of all twelve tribes and, far to the east, the Garden of Eden.

Geography, my father liked to explain, is a Greek word that means writing the world. A map will anchor you, ground you, guide you when you are lost. A map will supply the name of the town you are passing through and the stream running alongside the road.

My father knew the configuration of the earth not only as we understand it but as the ancients believed it to be.

He brought out primitive and astonishing maps, secreted in the volumes of his library. They showed the shape of the world and how it, incredibly, changed, from the Greek concept of the inhabited world to the Christian cosmos depicted by medieval monks to the approximation of our own charted by the great explorers.

My father would pull out *The World That Was,* the oversize blue book stuck in sideways beside the *Brockhaus,* and open it on the coffee table that stood in front of the couch.

"Sit, Julia," he would say.

I knew without my father telling me to keep my shoes off of the upholstery, but I knew he would remind me. The couch was green brocade, with a tall back, a carved frame, and threadbare armrests. It stood high off the floor and was firm to sit on. In my grandparents' apartment in Berlin, guests in formal clothes had perched on it stiffly, sipping after-dinner brandies.

"We won't get another one like it," my father said.

My father slid his fingers between the leaves of the book to find the place without bending the pages, which were old and fragile. He said we had to treat them carefully.

There were maps in the book made centuries ago, when the oceans were sailed and new lands discovered. Explorers plied the seas and then they charted them, not the other way around, explained my father, who never embarked on even the shortest journey without consulting timetables and maps.

They thought they knew how the world looked, and then they were completely surprised. For centuries, millennia, all time until then, the world was such and such and the next day, or week, or year, it was utterly changed, doubled in size, seas stretching farther than anyone had thought, though they had stretched far enough for sailors to lose themselves, even before.

"Imagine," my father said. "Imagine thinking that the world ends at Lake Michigan," which was three blocks away, just up Thorndale. You can't see across it, the water flows to the horizon. "Imagine you think it is the end of the world, and you can go no farther." He considered this for a moment. "That is what they thought when they looked across the Atlantic Ocean." Not across but out upon, for it too ended at a flat horizon, the ocean holding water like a cup holds a drink.

Together the Great Lakes, we learned in school, hold one-fifth of the fresh water on Earth. They formed at the end of the last Ice Age, when the glaciers melted into the huge depressions they had gouged in the earth.

My father turned the pages to show me how the maps had changed, one with just the barest outline of the American continents, quite empty and unfinished, and another, made decades later, almost filled in.

The first maps of North America didn't even show the Great Lakes. "They could have been drawn during the Ice Age!" He meant before the lakes were formed. On early maps of the newly found continent you can make out Florida, and the Maritimes, and Hudson's Bay. It was the seventeenth century before the lakes were "discovered" and explored by Europeans, and the eighteenth before they reliably appeared on maps.

The early maps had more space than markings, markings in just one corner, like scavenger-hunt charts. They showed slivers of continents and coastlines, forests with exotic animals, natives menacing or friendly. Delicate lines drifted off into nothingness.

The explorers set sail for they knew not where, venturing beyond that watery frontier which looks like a precipice. Sometimes they didn't know where they had landed, my father said. "Sometimes they got swallowed up, or shipwrecked, or eaten by savages." He laughed.

We'd learned about Columbus in school, and how he thought he had found India. "He never knew," my father said. "He went back three times and he never caught on!" My father would have figured out that he wasn't in India.

"It wasn't like going back for a schoolbook you've forgotten."

I didn't forget my schoolbooks, but Robbie did.

They crossed the ocean in little boats, my father explained, boats much, much smaller than the ship we took over, the *SS America*, tiny boats on the vast, stormy ocean. Their sails caught the wind. Sometimes the winds raged, ferocious squalls came up and tore the sails and blasted the boats off course. Enormous waves crashed over the sides and sometimes swamped the boats and sent them to the bottom of the sea. In the tropics the winds could die down and the boats lolled aimlessly in the doldrums, waiting for the breezes to blow again.

If they were lucky they found land before their food and water ran out.

"What if they didn't come back?" I asked.

"Getting back was easier," my father said. "They knew the way."

They could get lost, though, couldn't they? Even my

father said so. Shipwrecked or swallowed up. Maybe they got lost there, maybe they ran away. They could disappear, into forests where the sun never shines, on rivers going deeper and deeper into uncharted territory. Even if they made it ashore, even if they didn't get shipwrecked or blown off course.

A person could disappear, slip into the unknown. Never to be heard from again.

They are invisible, like dust motes in the dark. You thought you saw them but you couldn't be sure.

⊛⟨ 2 ⟩⊛

The day we left for America my father announced the time, and how long we had before the taxi arrived to load the luggage and take us to the train, which would carry us to Southampton, to the boat.

The trunks had been sent ahead, with the furniture. The piano, its legs disassembled, had been crated up, slid onto rollers and taken away.

My mother stood at the kitchen sink smoking a cigarette and looking out over the tiny back garden, a patch of grass with some roses, still wintering, along one side. She smoothed the narrow skirt of her beige traveling suit and adjusted the ankle strap of her new shoes. She picked up the rust-brown hat she'd bought for the journey and put it on in front of the mirror, adjusting her curls under the brim, turning it this way and that, taking it off again. She looked out the window again.

My grandmother Marta sat in the front parlor, her hair in a tight grey bun, her back set firmly against the chair slats, crocheting.

Marta had studied at the Berlin Conservatory and accompanied a famous violinist, his name now long forgotten, in the concert halls of central Europe. When they came to England Marta, still proud, wouldn't give lessons, even though they needed the money. Maybe because they needed the money. She never touched the piano again.

In Berlin there had been two pianos, one for my grandmother Marta to practice and give lessons on, the other for my mother, as there had been two buffets—the one we inherited and a bigger piece that my grandparents left behind when they fled.

Marta was not coming. Neither was my uncle Lewis, who in Germany had been called Ludwig and seemed still to be expecting a blow, verbal or otherwise.

My father watched the clock to make sure we didn't miss the moment of departure.

"Thirty-two minutes," my father called out. "Robbie, where are you?" And, to my mother, "Perhaps we should call the taxi, to make sure."

"They'll be here in half an hour."

When the taxi came we had to be ready. The driver would walk up the path, along the flagstones that curved narrowly through the front garden, to the porch. My father would have noticed him already, a middle-aged man wearing a chauffeur's cap and leather driving gloves. The man would never have to raise his hand to the bell, wouldn't wait in the doorway under the porch roof. By that time my father would have opened the door and placed the suitcases on the porch, the first ones, for the man to lift and take down and load into the cab.

Robbie was going to have to start a new school and leave his mates and our street, where he had just gotten old enough to go out and play without my mother having to watch him, and find his friends and kick the ball and watch out for cars. There weren't many cars on our street, people didn't own so many cars in those days. We didn't have one either. But the street curved, so it was difficult to see the cars. They could come up all of a sudden.

Things will be different in America, my father told us. There won't be as much rain, but there will be snow. Snow comes when the atmosphere above is cold. Crystals form in the clouds and float down. If you look at the crystals each one is different. I didn't remember snow, though Robbie did. It had snowed two winters before, five inches, extraordinary.

In Chicago we'll see plenty of snow. He'll show us the crystals, they're beautiful. They had snow in Germany when he was a boy, but in America there will be even more than that. Chill winds blow all across the continent and down from Canada. The winds need miles and miles to gather their strength. Not the wind we could feel on our faces but winds high up in the atmosphere that carry the weather.

Perhaps we'd see snow when we arrive, but most likely we won't. It will be April. We'll probably have to wait until next year. In London the days were beginning to warm, you could see little buds on the roses, but it's much colder in Chicago.

"It won't be like here in England." A cool rain surrounded our island, made our atmosphere. Not rain like in the jungle, which I had a book about, where plants grew huge, glossy, many-lobed leaves that fanned out everywhere. In England the rain misted gently, droplets clung to the blades of grass, the branches and stalks and the garden chairs that never got brought in because there was no place to put them.

Today the sun shone brilliantly. It was March, and cold. We posed for photographs against the bare wisteria climbing the front porch, Robbie and I in our matching new pea coats, my mother wearing a camel coat with a fox collar that had the fox still in it.

First my parents posed, then the two of them with Robbie and me, Lewis added, then subtracted, and Marta. My father and Lewis took turns with the camera.

My father wears a dark, pin-striped, double-breasted suit, a handkerchief carefully folded in the pocket. With his high forehead and thin, long, angular face, he looks taller than he was. He stands perfectly composed, his eyes leveled at the camera, his dignified half-smile giving nothing away.

My mother looks worried, pained perhaps, though trying to smile. She pulls the fur collar up around her neck, against her face. The sun is shining brightly. Maybe she is only squinting into the glare.

On a globe in the library of the *SS America*, my father showed Robbie and me where we had come from.

A giant floating ball suspended in a wooden stand, the globe turned on its axis and tilted up and down. Robbie twirled it, blurring the colors.

The globe came almost to my father's waist. He let the ball slow. "How blue it is," he said. "Most of the earth is water, you see—the ocean we're traveling on right now." He studied the surface. "How many have sailed as we are today?"

We could see where we started and where we were going.

Robbie couldn't find it, couldn't find England.

"It's an island."

"I know that," Robbie sulked, pulled back, then let my father show him.

It was small, a blot of color near the top. My father tipped the sphere so I could see. He traced his finger leftward across the blue, a far way, it looked. "We're about here," he said, pointing to a spot in the ocean. Robbie crept forward behind my father, wanting to see but not to show it.

My father rotated the ball slowly in the other direction than Robbie had twirled it, the opposite way you would naturally turn it. The earth goes this way, my father said.

"Why?" Robbie asked.

"Ah, why," my father smiled. "Who can say why?"

The globe was a beautiful thing spinning or not, spinning with shimmery colors and forms or still with vast azure waters and curiously shaped pieces of land, mountains rising across continents and strung like necklaces along seacoasts.

"Down here is the tropic of Cancer," my father said, stopping the spin, pointing near the maroon band at the center, the equator, where the sun hits the waters directly, warming them, sending them flowing northeast.

We'll sail past the Grand Banks, my father told us, with its powerful storms and bountiful fish.

My father explained how the Gulf Stream carried warm tropical waters across the Atlantic, under the very place we were sailing now. So that England, up here—he pointed—was much much milder than Chicago. Currents we couldn't see decided everything, my father said: where it is habitable to live, the vegetation, the climate. That's what keeps us warm and moist at home—in England, he corrected. It wasn't home now.

He let Robbie find Chicago, amidst a wide flat land, no mountains anywhere near. There was water, though, my father said, showing us the long finger of Lake Michigan, a drop out of the seas, of the blue washing everywhere.

Outside the waters churned angry and grey—not aquamarine like the globe. The ship rocked in the choppiness, and my mother didn't come out of the cabin.

◈{ 3 }◈

By the time we arrived in Chicago, the weather was warm.

The moving van stopped in the alley behind the building, but it blocked the delivery entrance of the Kroger supermarket, so someone told the men to move it, and then they parked on Thorndale. I didn't know the names of the streets yet, or what the front of the Kroger's looked like.

My brother stood by the street-side fence watching the movers unload the truck.

I noticed a girl through the trees in the next yard, on a swing. She looked about my age.

There was a fence between us, with trees and bushes that parted just enough so I could see the spiral stripes along the poles, the motion of the swing as it passed the open place, and the girl on it. She had dark hair in bangs and a round contented face. She whooshed up and back, up and back.

I explored the backyard, counting my steps along the walkway that split it into two grassy squares. I followed the edge of the pebbly pavement, sticking out my arms for balance, from the stairway to the back fence. At the fence

I curled my fingers around the wire. A car went down the alley, kind of fast.

I caught glances through the trees, but if the girl looked back I turned away.

The movers lifted the furniture out of the truck and set it on the grass. One was tall and shirtless, a kerchief tied around his neck, his skin glistening with sweat, the other shorter, with muscles bulging out of his T-shirt and eyes that stared wide out of their sockets.

The tall one spoke some foreign tongue, a sing-song; the other muttered back. They picked up the sofa end-by-end and eased it through the gate. Robbie followed to the stairway, stood behind them as they started up, the tall one first, backwards, lifting the sofa high. They pulled and turned it like a puzzle piece, snaking around the corners, barely resting on the landings.

Robbie kept a few steps below until, just before they reached our floor, they stopped, and Robbie, still climbing, bumped into the second man, the one with the eyes, then turned and ran. He came racing down the stairs, went out the gate and disappeared behind the side of the building.

The movers came down and took the marble top off the buffet and set it against the wheels of the moving van. They raised the buffet between them and carried it into the yard and up the stairs. It was heavy, even without the china. I saw my brother creep around the corner and follow them, a few steps behind.

The men hoisted the piano on ropes outside the

stairway, eased it over the railing and onto the landing. Robbie went inside just ahead of the piano. I came up too and followed them down the hallway to the living room, where they put the piano on its side and screwed in the fat round legs. Then they righted it and placed it in the little half-room all the way in front, with windows all around and the black-and-white tiles on the floor. The sun streamed in.

Back in the kitchen my mother filled some water glasses for the movers.

"Thank you, ma'am," the tall one said, mopping his brow with a handkerchief. So they did speak English.

Our apartment was laid out like the Larsens' below us and the Ewens' across the hall, like Molly's on the other side of Thorndale and Rachel's over on Kenmore. It was a Chicago six-flat, the standard.

You came in by the back porch, which was wood and we used for storage and to hang laundry sometimes. Then you opened the door to the kitchen, where the linoleum was worn and the sink hung off the wall. In the breadbox you could find rye and pumpernickel, and in the refrigerator Liederkranz and mettwurst and hard salami.

From the kitchen you swung the door to the dining room, with three windows along one side and off the dining room my brother's room, and, if you kept going, the long dark hallway. Off the hallway was the bathroom with its big tub on feet and on the other side the telephone closet with the crumbling wall and the heavy black phone. At the end of the hall was the foyer and the door that company came in, and opposite that the master bedroom and on the other side my room and at an angle the opening to the living room and in the very front the sun porch with the piano.

In the morning I would bring two of my dolls—Millicent and Elizabeth, Milly and Silly I called them—into the kitchen and sit them on chairs, next to my mother.

She wore a woolen bathrobe with grey and blue checks that felt rough against my skin and smelled of England.

She looked up as I came alongside her. She didn't read the newspaper all the time like my father and pretend not to notice when people spoke. She read books, and smiled, or raised her head and stared in a dreamy far-off way, but if you tapped her hand she came back.

I served my dolls tea out of the set my aunt Runia gave me the day we left England. Runia was my uncle Lewis's fiancée. She and Lewis were going to get married after we left and made room in the house for them.

Later I would bring *Bartholomew and the Oobleck* into the living room, and my mother would push back into the cushions of the sofa, and I'd push back too, settling against her.

I turned the pages and looked at the pictures.

"Why did the king want oobleck?" I asked.

"Because he's not satisfied with what he's always had."

"Why didn't he like the oobleck, if he asked for it?"

"Because it was sticky and covered everything. He didn't know that's what he was going to get."

"Read it again," I'd say, but she'd laugh and close the book, and I'd carry it back to my room. I told it to myself, hearing her echo.

She'd make my lunch and clear the table and stand at the kitchen sink washing the dishes.

I'd come up behind her and curl my fingers around the sash circling her waist, holding the dress where a button was missing. She kept untying it and closing it again, saying she must get around to fixing it.

I put my face against her front, felt the rising and falling, caught the same breaths.

Outside my window the catalpa trees waved their enormous leaves and dropped long brown pods over the ground. They spread their shade over the narrow street lined with six-flat apartment houses like ours and a few single-families like the one next door. The other end of the block was a long way off.

I met the girl on the swing, and we visited back and forth. Her name was Ginger. Now I could swing too.

We played hopscotch and dolls.

At Ginger's we fed our dolls out of a thimble and put them to bed on the sofa cushions.

At my house I lined up my dolls on the living-room rug, in rows that followed the carpet pattern, front to back like at our school. Milly and Silly bent at the waist and could sit. Marcie couldn't, so I propped her against a chair leg to keep her from falling down. Rosemary was slim and grown-up, with glistening blond waves and a silky red shirtwaist and a belt that buckled. I stood her as the teacher in front of the class.

Ginger brought Josie and Gwendolyn and sat them on the carpet.

The pupils took turns reading aloud. We stood them up one by one while I held the book. If they faltered we helped them.

We chased lightning bugs as the day faded and disappeared, but we had not yet been called in. We swooped our jars into the shadows to catch them.

The pavement rode rough under our roller skates, the skate key swinging on a string around my neck. We stepped down carefully from the curb, looked to both sides, then crossed the street. It was smoother than the sidewalk, and bowed up in the center.

We walked to school along Thorndale, across the alley and past the yellow brick of the Kroger's. At Broadway the patrol boy, an eighth-grader with a white sash across his chest, held out his arms. Trucks lumbered past and streetcars screeched along their tracks. Finally the light changed and he let us by.

On the other side of Broadway we caught the warm sweet smells of the bakery. We passed the long, glassy, jet-black front of Pat's Bar, only a small opening, not quite a window, too high for me to see into. Then under the El past the murkiness, the station entrance across the street, always dark and damp. We walked a little faster there. Finally we reached the iron fence beside the playground and followed it around.

At school we had *Fun with Dick and Jane,* arithmetic, and spelling between hard frayed covers, with the names of long-gone pupils scrawled in the grid inside.

Words floated on the page, swam up, linked together, started to mean something. On large brownish wide-lined sheets we shaped our letters, here round, there straight, follow the cards above the blackboard, though mine never looked like those. We kept crayon boxes inside our desks for illustrations. I liked words better.

After school I did my homework, the little we had. My mother watched while I wrote out my spelling words. They were easy I thought.

She thought English spelling was hard. But "Arithmetic's the same everywhere," she said when I did my sums. "Except for your father!"

Three bleats of the school bell meant an air-raid drill. We had to close our readers and put them away. Miss Conway inspected to see we cleared our desks.

We marched row by row, single file, slipped under the slides where we hung our coats and hunkered, backs to the windows, heads down.

Miss Conway took the pole, closed the windows and pulled the shades. "No talking!"

We practiced, got good at it, calm as the teacher, waiting for the all-clear.

And what if a bomb dropped, here, on Chicago?

I brought home colds, swollen glands, childhood illnesses, "one after another," as my father liked to say. If I was sick I could stay home, and my mother heated up milk and poured in honey, and it slid down my throat. She sat beside me on the bed. She laid her palm on my forehead, on my tummy. She felt my breathing, and I felt hers.

I tucked my dolls under the covers with me and gave them milk with honey, too, in the little teacups.

In the morning my father would go into the kitchen to make his tea and boil his egg and toast his bread and put it in the toast rack we brought from England, which was tarnished and bent, with two of the prongs sprung from the base, and butter it and spread on Crosse and Blackwell marmalade from a jar that seemed English too but wasn't.

He sat at the table with his newspaper folded in front of him, holding it in his left hand, reading the headlines or the sports page. He drank a small glass of grapefruit juice poured out of a can pierced on the top in two places. It had to be done that way, it was a matter of physics.

He left carrying a newspaper under his arm and a furled, swan-handled black umbrella in his hand.

When he came home at night he changed from his suit into slacks and a shirt and jacket, like a suit jacket but loose-fitting corduroy or tweed. He wore a jacket except when it was hot. He sat down in his chair in the living room with his newspaper, and later my mother gave him supper, but it was after we already had eaten because we ate something hot at night but he didn't, he had a hot meal during the day, at the hospital. It's the proper way to eat, the main meal at midday, he said.

Refugees like us who wound up in Chicago came once in a while for dinner.

They rang the bell and came up the cool, musty inner staircase, where a little runner of rug led to each apartment door. The stairway held a quiet, dark scent, not exactly of food and not of mildew. Of being closed in, a passage.

They spoke of Berlin, of skiing trips and schoolmasters, hikes in the Alps, and the village where they stopped that had a certain kind of cheese.

"Do you remember the taste?" recalled Max Blaubender. "There is nothing like it."

"I have found it at Stop and Shop," said Dorothea Stern. "They import it from Austria."

"I wouldn't buy from Austria, would you?" put in Lotte Feuerstein.

"Too sweet, those Viennese," said Max.

"But the schlag!"

"Schlag better be sweet," said my father.

If I wanted to stay up, I had to say hello, greet them as they came in and took off their coats and looked around, maybe for the best seat? They rang the bell and came up the front way.

Dorothea Stern was thin and angular, with very short hair. Still, her husband disappeared behind her.

Hilde Blaubender had red hair, wore a shimmery dress cut deep in front, and jangled bracelets on her wrist. Max was in furs. Max's mother had been a patient of my grandfather. I don't think in Berlin they would have been invited, but in Chicago these refugees stuck together.

The Feuersteins, Emil and Lotte, seemed more like my parents. He was a professor, tall and wiry, with a craggy face and clever words. Lotte didn't talk unless she had something to say.

My father talked to the men in the living room while the women went down the hallway to the kitchen.

I noticed their accents and the way they carried themselves, heads up. They jumped from English to German and back again.

My mother wore her red velvet dress with puff sleeves she said was too fancy but my father liked, it made her look all delicate, or sometimes a pale blue that set off her eyes. She tied on an apron, saying, "I only have this dress," even though she had another. "I better be careful!" Things were cooking on the stove, in the oven. "It's hot, don't touch, be careful." We always were being careful in our house. Things bubbled in pots, giving off smells sour or sweet, I wasn't sure, maybe both.

She stood at the table, she had to bend down to stir whatever it was. "This is worse than the kitchen in England," she laughed. "There we had no kitchen at all!" I wasn't sure any more if that was so. She mixed and added milk, flour, salt, and pepper, showering them into the bowl, sprinkled parsley off the tips of her fingers. She shaped, rounded, patted, her touch light and easy.

"Kartoffel kloesse," she said.

I tried to pronounce it.

"Luckily you don't have to learn," she said, placing them on a plate, each one after she formed it.

"They're beautiful," I said.

She laughed. "They're only potatoes."

Tonight she wouldn't tuck the covers around me and sit on the edge of the bed and lean down, hands on either side, and kiss me on the forehead. She wouldn't sit there, like she usually did, so quietly I could hear her breathing and time my breaths and listen till I thought I could hear them together, and then somehow I didn't hear anything because I had fallen asleep.

Tonight her laughter faded down the hallway, mixing with, stirred under by that of her guests. I could hear voices from the dining room though not words, louder then softer, rising in the distance like a wave heading for shore, crashing, then pausing, swelling again. A sliver of light cut across my bed, the door wasn't shut all the way. I tossed from one side to the other, pajamas bunching around me. I turned and turned, back and forth on my pillow which grew warm so I turned it too, until finally I could hear the voices no more.

In the summer we played in front, on Magnolia, me and my friends, Ginger next door and Molly from across the street, and Charlotte, who lived down Broadway. Broadway was a wide commercial avenue with streetcars and traffic.

The mothers sat on our top step, watching as we played hopscotch and Simon Says and Red Rover, Cross Over on the sidewalk in front of our building or next door at Ginger's.

My mother wouldn't come out in slippers, the mules she wore around the house, but in yellow straw sandals with wedge heels, the coolest shoes she had. It was hot in Chicago, she hadn't expected it. Her housedress she didn't change, but she wouldn't let people see her in slippers.

Leila, Ginger's mother, came out and sat with my mother, then my mother would go over to their steps, not a stoop really, because it was a regular house. Leila didn't wear housedresses, and her hair was always perfectly combed.

Some days my mother stuffed towels and sandwiches into a brown checked bag and we walked to the beach, usually the one at the end of Thorndale, which was tucked between buildings. Sometimes we went along Sheridan Road, which followed the lake, a few more blocks to Hollywood, where the sand was wider and the lifeguard sat at the top of a tall white tower. It was a long walk, I thought, and hard for me to keep up. Robbie's friends were at Hollywood and it was my fault, my slowness and tiredness and my legs that would not carry me, when we didn't get that far.

Hollywood was better if I could make it, because then Robbie went off to play ball with his friends and race them into the water.

When we arrived, my mother pulled an old thin blue blanket out of her bag and handed me a corner of it. I grabbed the ravelly edge and helped her pull this way and that till it lay smooth over the sand. We put our shoes on the four corners to hold it down.

She lay down on the blanket, propping herself on some folded towels, a book in her hands. "Let me see you swim," she said, as I stepped through the sand to the water.

The sand shifted under my feet, squirted up between my toes. Sometimes it was hot, too hot, and I had to step fast to get to the cool part where the waves came up.

The water lapped in, splashing high against my legs. I looked back at her as I went deeper, got wet. I pretended to swim, watching other kids who did. I paddled but sank, had to put my feet down, went up on tiptoes as a wave came, liked the feel of it, cool.

When I came out of the water, dripping, my mother wrapped me in a big yellow towel and pulled me to her, rubbing my shivering arms, and held me.

On weekends sometimes my father came with us, but he hated the sand in things and the flies that came. He carried canvas chairs for him and my mother and she stretched out, easy, warming her feet in the sand. We had to keep smoothing the blanket and not bother him when he was reading. He was allergic to the cold water, it gave him hives, and the lake was icy, though I didn't mind. He told me about the shells and stones I found.

Sometimes I saw my mother staring way off into the distance, farther even than across the lake—which you couldn't see anyway, not across Lake Michigan, it's like the ocean.

⟨ 4 ⟩

Before school started again we went to visit my grandparents on the Denver Zephyr, a sleek silvery train that ran overnight from Chicago.

The Denver Zephyr had huge wheels and high entrances that you needed special portable steps to reach, even if you were a grownup. The trainman put down the steps and held out his hand to help you. The Denver Zephyr went every day in each direction, traveling at night and arriving in the morning.

It pulled out of Union Station in Chicago in the evening. In the summer it was still light, the light lasted a long time. Then the twilight began to lengthen the shadows and slant the sun into the windows.

The train traveled with magnificent speed and smoothness despite the clackety-clack and the wobbling and teetering of people maneuvering in the aisles. Not us, we were children, it was a ride in an amusement park, where I had never been. We didn't go to places like amusement parks or bowling alleys. We packed our clothes into worn leather valises plastered with emblems of European travel which the porter loaded into the luggage compartment, except for the overnight case my mother carried, a train case she called it, and a small suitcase for my father, which had our pajamas and slippers and a change of clothing for the next day, when my grandparents would meet us at the station in Denver.

Inside the seats were plush but everything else was shiny and hard. At bedtime they folded up the seats, pulled the beds down from the wall, and drew the green curtains closed. In the middle of the night I woke from the stopping at Omaha, Nebraska, to see darkness outside, a lone streetlight, and a single baggage truck being wheeled along the platform. In the morning we had breakfast in the dining car, with flowers in a thin vase, wet silvery pitchers sweating onto white cloth, and the waiter pouring my milk.

Denver is the mile-high city, exactly 5,280 feet, but it towers over nothing, it's the western edge of a slowly elevating plain. It looks as flat as it can be. What do you cross but space, with grasses and corn and wheat and the occasional road and farmhouse and crossroads that fly by faster than you can see them.

The Denver Zephyr traveled on tracks laid in the eighteen-seventies and -eighties with the sweat of indentured workers from China and Hungary and Italy, who put down the wooden ties and steel tracks of the transcontinental railroad. They laid it as straight as they could. It isn't difficult to follow a straight line from Chicago to Denver.

Denver is marked on the map with a star, it's the state capital. You can see the capitol there, grey and sturdy, though I've never been inside. We went to Springfield to see the Illinois state capital with my father, later, driving through cornfields. Springfield is a small town, but the capitol is grand. Denver is much bigger than Springfield and smaller than Chicago. It also has streets that go on and on, straight and plain. The mountains rise in the west, along the horizon, but they look small. You have to get close to see how enormous they are. They're a blister on the globe, a sudden brown along the lefthand side of the map.

My grandparents' apartment was stuffed with pieces of furniture they had brought from Europe, just as we had brought ours. They lived above a grocery store, as we lived behind one. Ours was a supermarket, though. Their apartment was smaller than ours, more cramped, with dark armoires, flowery armchairs, and tables covered with lace cloths.

Grandfather Friedrich stood straight-backed and wore a suit and tie. The smooth pink dome of his head reflected the light. With a great beak of a nose, he looked like one of the eagles my father said we might see when we went up to the mountains. We would have to look hard. We had packed opera glasses.

My grandmother, Minna, was small and dark-haired, which seemed odd. She asked a lot of questions, not all of which I could understand, and didn't listen for the answers. She patted my father on the back, which I had never seen anyone do. He pretended not to notice.

Minna kept the curtains drawn, heavy curtains they were against the bright harsh mountain sun, to prevent the carpets and upholstery from fading any more than they had already. My grandmother moved around the apartment quietly, behind the curtains. You needed to be quiet in grandparents' apartment.

My grandmother Minna spoke to my grandfather in German and wouldn't let anyone enter the tiny kitchen, where she distractedly prepared our lunch—dinner she called it, the main meal, served from paper-thin china. She brought out the serving dishes, each with its lid, and grandfather served.

"Minna, how much trouble have you gone to," my mother said.

"Not at all," said Minna, not seeming to mean it.

My grandmother had baked a plumcake because we had come such a long way and it was so unusual to see us. Rows of plum slices ran lengthwise on the cake, deep red and glistening with juices released by the sugar and the baking. It was tart and sweet at the same time.

Minna ran a long silver knife between the rows, then sliced across, delicately lifted each small square with a pearl-handled spatula and placed it on a plate. She served Friedrich first and then my father, passing cake forks, but Friedrich passed his piece to my mother saying, with a mock American accent, "Ladies first." Robbie ate the crust but left the plums on the plate. I finished my piece and wanted more. Prune plums ripen at the end of summer.

Friedrich had been wounded in the war, not the war my parents sometimes talked about but the one before that. He was in the medical corps and operating, in a tent just behind the lines, when a stray bullet pierced his thigh. While recovering from his wounds, which were superficial but slow to mend, Friedrich watched men injured much more seriously than he was, bandaged, hobbling on crutches or with clumsy wooden legs. He considered the problem of how to repair the terrible maimings that were commonplace in trench warfare. With pen and ink he created lighter, more graceful limbs. When he was discharged Friedrich returned to his practice in Berlin with designs for new kinds of prostheses that, with an old school chum who owned a machine-tool factory, he began to manufacture out of materials invented for airplanes. Friedrich expanded his medical practice to treat some of the war's many, many wounded men and hired two nurses to show them how to attach and remove their new limbs and exercises to become adept in their use.

My grandfather used to take my father down to his office, on the ground floor of their apartment building, and show him the limbs he fitted for his patients. My father wanted to know what happened to their regular legs, and how much blood was shed. On the prescription pad my grandfather gave him, my father worked out mathematical problems he thought up in the afternoons after finishing his homework—like how much air there was in their apartment or the number of leaves on the beech tree in the backyard. My father wanted to study mathematics at university, but my grandfather didn't believe he could make a living as a mathematician and insisted he study medicine instead.

Friedrich knew a lodge high up in the mountains, among the wildflowers. It was like the Alps, maybe even more beautiful. A car would take us.

I had special new clothes—blue jeans that were too big for me, rolled up wide at the cuffs, and a flannel shirt that looked like a cowboy's. I would have to wear my brown oxfords, which my father said were the only decent shoes in America. Did I want the rattlesnakes to get me?

My father had brought his hiking boots, which he'd last worn climbing the Jungfrau, in 1932. "It was threatening rain," he told us, "and we made it in record time."

"What's the record?" Robbie asked.

"Not an official record, you see," my father said. "Only very fast."

But on the day, instead of us all going to the mountains, my father and mother went out early. They left before Robbie and I were up, and didn't come back until late.

When they returned my mother lay down in my grandparents' bedroom, because my parents' bed was the living-room couch.

In the evening my father asked whether we would lose our deposit at the lodge, and was the car company going to charge us too? He spoke of tests, delays, which day we might go, how long we could stay. He studied the calendar, folded and unfolded a map.

"Eric," my grandfather said, "these are only details."

"We made plans months ago," my father replied.

My mother said, "You go, I'm too much trouble," but my father replied, "Nonsense." Still, he didn't stop discussing the arrangements.

When the phone call came, my father put the receiver down, satisfied.

"Everything's fine," he told Friedrich. "Negative, Eve. Negative."

"What's 'negative'?" I asked.

"Nothing," my father said.

By then it was too late for our expedition, we had return tickets on the train.

My mother was quiet, staring out of the train window.

"You will come back and see the mountains," she said.

II
Stones

⊛{ 5 }⊛

My father wasn't supposed to be sitting in the kitchen, in the suit he wore to work, at three o'clock when I came home from school.

My father never was home in the afternoon, neither were any of the other fathers I knew. Ginger's wasn't, he came home after we were done with our games and I had gone home. Molly's father didn't go to an office, he went to a plant, the kind where they make things, and he came home earlier but not till dinnertime.

My father didn't speak just as he didn't speak in the morning when I got up or in the evening when he sat down with his newspaper and sometimes fell asleep even before he had supper. He'd shake when my mother woke him up to tell him supper was ready.

My father seemed to see everything, underneath or through. But now he looked at me, then away from me, as if I wasn't there.

My mother came out of their bedroom wearing her best dress, not the fanciest but the newest, the one she'd brought home one day and held up in front of the mirror saying, "Isn't it American?" It was stiff, navy-blue material with a cinched waist and white star-shaped buttons. It was hard to the touch.

She dressed up for the opera or a party, more dressed than this, but not in the daytime, not in the afternoon.

She was carrying the neat, square train case she'd taken on the Denver Zephyr with lingerie and makeup, slippers and the clothes she would wear to meet my grandparents in the morning—more than you'd think would fit.

My mother stood there not like my mother but a woman going out, already on her way.

"Where?" I asked, and she opened her mouth, but he spoke first.

"Eve, put the bag down," my father told her.

"It isn't heavy," she said.

"Everything is heavy now."

He looked at his watch and said, "Mrs. Ewen will be here any minute."

"Mrs. Ewen?" I asked.

"From across the hall. To stay with you."

"Why?"

"A child your age can't stay alone."

The doorbell rang.

My mother let my father take the case out of her hand, as he said, "The taxi's here."

"Be good," she said, leaning to kiss me, I thought, but my father took her arm and said, "They'll be waiting for us."

They went out the front door, just as Mrs. Ewen came in.

I watched them from my window, through the catalpas. I caught sight of my father's suit and the blue dress, stiff and sharp, as my mother got into the taxi, not looking up. The cab pulled away from the curb and headed down the street.

We didn't have a car then. We took the El downtown or the bus down Broadway to Bryn Mawr, to the Stop and Shop where my mother got the German sausage my father liked and cheese that smelled funny. Once we took a train out to the country and visited someone my father knew, and played on a wide sloping lawn and could see cornfields in the distance. We took a taxi to the train station then, and also when we went to Colorado, and when we arrived home, in the evening, tired and with all our bags, my father didn't let my mother carry anything then either. I'd forgotten but now I remembered.

Mrs. Ewen sat in the living room, reading a magazine. She had grey hair with a net around it, and she sat very still and seemed to be trying not to look up. Mrs. Ewen didn't have children, or maybe her children were grown and gone, but I never saw children with her, and she usually didn't speak when she saw us in the yard or on the stairs.

Robbie came home, pounding the baseball against his mitt, pretending I wasn't there. He went into his room and shut the door. I could hear the ball against the wall. My mother would have told him to stop.

I went to Robbie's door and flapped my hand against

it, but if it made a sound it got lost within the pounding of the ball he continued to throw against the wall, or started throwing again it seemed to me once I started to knock. He never let me in anyway, didn't want girl contaminating his things.

The floor creaked along the hallway, and the ball seemed to stop. There was silence except for my own steps, which didn't seem like mine. The hallway was long and shadowy with my room at the end of it, by the front door where they had left from. All the apartments had a hallway like this. The other apartments were the same shape, except some were backwards, and they had different furniture and smells.

Either I couldn't hear the ball or he had stopped. I left my door open. There were groans along the hallway still, but no one.

"Bet you don't know where she went," Robbie said. We were sitting at the dining-room table, where Mrs. Ewen had given us dinner.

"I didn't say that."

"It's true, though."

"What'll you give me to tell you?" he said.

"I don't have anything."

"Sure you do. The silver dollar Opa gave you, for instance. Or don't you remember?"

"'Course I do."

"The silver dollar—"

"I put it in my piggy bank."

"Hand it over."

Grandfather Friedrich had taken the silver dollar out of a box, a very special box that sat on the desk in his office, what he called his office, which was a corner of their living room.

It was the day we were supposed to go to the mountains, the day after my mother and father had gone out in the morning and not come back till late. He had taken me to the park, and when we came back my mother was lying down on my grandparents' bed, and Grandfather said, "Come, Julia, let me show you something."

It was a small wooden box with three drawers, each with a little brass knob. Out of the top drawer he pulled keys on a leather chain, which he said were the keys to their apartment on Uhlandstrasse, Number 179. That, he said, was in a place far, far away. He made as if to turn one of the keys in a lock.

Out of the second drawer he took a small pad of paper, which had his name printed at the top and the word *Arzt,* which he said meant doctor. It was a pad to write an order for medicine. When my father was just a little older than me, Grandfather said, he used to play with such a pad, and work out problems, like the amount of water that could fit in the bathtub.

"That's silly," I said.

"Yes, I suppose it was," he said, "but your father always liked numbers best."

He tore off one of the sheets and gave it to me.

"It's from a long time ago. You can write or draw on it if you want, but maybe you'll put it away and take it out some day, and it will be even older then than it is now."

He opened the third drawer and took out some coins. Some of them were very big and some were tiny, and some weren't round but had straight edges all around, like a stop sign. He took out a silver dollar, like the one he and my grandmother had sent me for my birthday. It was large and shiny. He was about to put it back and close the drawer, but he put it in my hand instead.

"Here's a little something extra," he said. "Insurance."

"What's insurance?" I asked.

"Something, as they say here in America, for a rainy day."

I put the paper and the silver dollar in a pocket in my suitcase, where Robbie wouldn't find them.

I went to my room and pulled the piggy bank off the bookshelf. It was a mailbox, with a slot where you put the money in and a keyhole where you opened it.

I didn't want to give it to Robbie, so I walked slow.

"Let's go," he called.

He opened it and emptied out the change, a small pile of pennies and nickels mostly. Two silver dollars.

"What a sorry stash," he said, picking out the large coins.

"You said one!"

"One or two, what's the diff?" He tried out their weight in his cupped hand, put one in each.

"You said one."

"Do you want to know, or not?"

"Opa gave me those."

"So, he'll give you another. Next year."

"Tell me!"

"She's in the hospital."

"The hospital?"

"Now you know." He got up, stretching his leg, shoving the silver dollars into his pants pocket.

"What's she doing there?"

"She's gonna have an operation." I looked at him.

"It's where they cut you open." He sat down again.

"I knew that."

"No, you didn't. You don't know where, either."

He waited for me to say it.

"Right here." He ran his hand across my belly. "With a knife, a real sharp knife, sharper than any we've got. Right across the middle."

"What for?"

"To take something out. Why else?"

"How do you know?"

"I heard Dad talking about it."

"He told you that?"

"He told me some of it."

"What do they take out?"

"I didn't hear that part." Now he got up quick, turned

for his door, went inside and closed it. He was hiding the silver dollars, for sure.

◈ 6 ◈

In the morning my father called out twice or even three times, although twice would have been once too many. He did not want to be there, at the doorway to my room. It was not fitting.

My father stood with the newspaper under his arm.

"Eight-twenty-five," he said. "We're leaving at eight-twenty-five. You have to get ready."

My mother would have come in and sat on the edge of the bed, touching my shoulder, whispering *Julia*, tiptoeing into my sleep. Wouldn't she? Mothers sit where you can feel them against you and know they are there before you open your eyes.

"Julia, hurry," my father called.

I held onto my dolls under the covers.

She would have my bathrobe in her hands, waiting, and help me put it on. Mine was getting tight, I needed a new one.

"If you don't get up we'll have to leave you here."

My mother would sit at the edge of the bed. I could hear her breath even before I opened my eyes. *Julia, Julia, it's time to get up,* she'd whisper, touching my shoulder, laughing a little as she did.

I would pretend to still be sleeping but I'd already be

awake or half awake, trying to keep my eyes closed, keeping a smile from my face because then she could tell, even if I didn't open my eyes.

My father said, "Get up, get up, it's eight," and "I'm going to come in."

I got out of bed as he came into the room.

"Where are your clothes?" he asked. He opened the closet door.

My mother handed me my clothes in the morning. She helped me get them on.

I went into the closet and found a blouse and a skirt, which cut around the waist.

My father poured cereal into my bowl, splashed in the milk, gave me a spoon that was too big. I could hardly get it in my mouth, it was a trouble to change it. He kept glancing at the clock while I ate, watching each spoonful scooped up and carried to my mouth, quick and careful as I could, some of the flakes spilling.

His cuffs were folded up, his jacket and tie draped over a dining-room chair, waiting.

"That's a nice outfit," Robbie said when he came out. "Stripes and checks. I saw a clown like that in the circus."

I looked down at myself, got up to change. Maybe I could find something else. But my father said, "Now! It's eight-twenty, we have to go."

I couldn't snap my barrette, so I pushed the hair back behind my ear, but it kept slipping out.

"Wait for her after school," my father said to Robbie

when we left in the morning. "Go upstairs together."

I wasn't supposed to walk home by myself, my brother was supposed to go with me, which he hated doing. He'd walk as fast as he could, so I could hardly keep up, though he'd stop at Broadway where there's a patrol boy because he knew he had to wait for me there. That's the only street we had to cross.

At the gate to our backyard he would let me go ahead and up the stairs. Then he was free for his games.

Inside my mother would be standing at the kitchen sink, and bend down and hug me. I could feel the softness, her dress and her.

She would put out cookies on the table and pour the milk.

Milk is cold going down and even in your stomach.

Or she would be standing at the counter chopping or sitting at the table reading a book or a magazine. She said magazines were silly, but sometimes she bought one at the Kroger's.

She would let go of the chopping or washing or reading and sit beside me.

Still she could be dreaming, thinking, wandering in her mind.

"Mommy," I'd say, waking her up, and she'd say, "I was off somewhere."

Now Robbie went into the yard and up the stairs ahead of me. When I got to the top he was at the back door. He had a key. He hunched over so I couldn't watch. He was trying to fit the key into the lock. He turned it this way and that before he got the door open.

I followed him into the kitchen.

"Where's Mommy?" I asked.

"Don't you remember anything?"

Some afternoons Mrs. Ewen came over and sat in the easy chair turning the pages of her magazine. It seemed to always be the same one.

Sometimes we had a babysitter. They were even older than Mrs. Ewen. They sat in the dining room, where I usually did my homework. They'd lean over my spelling book to say how hard it looked, or ask what I was writing. I didn't like them sitting there.

Usually I went to a friend's house after school, especially Ginger's. I had to wait for my father to pick me up. If it got late Leila started cooking dinner, and looking at the clock. Sometimes Mel, Ginger's father, got home before my father arrived. Maybe I'd stay for dinner, and then my father would get there and I'd have to leave in the middle, the food half-finished on my plate.

She went away, my father said, so she could get better.

"What's wrong with her?"

"Nothing."

In a comic book Robbie had shown me how they slipped poison into a glass of tea, and the hero turned green. He said he'd do it to me if I wasn't careful.

"Poisoned?" my father said, angry, when I asked. "Poisoned?"

❧ 7 ❧

At school they sent home a notice, which I folded into my notebook. My mother signed them and I'd hand them back in. She'd make a note in her diary and remember when the day came.

"We're going to Hawthorn Mellody Farm," Mrs. Dermott announced. "We'll see cows being milked.

"It's next Tuesday," she said, pointing to the date on the calendar hanging next to the blackboard. "Make sure your mother signs the permission slip, and bring it back tomorrow."

"I got something for Mommy," I told my father when he got home.

"Be good, and she'll be home soon," he said.

"We're going on a field trip, to a farm. Mommy has to sign the slip."

He headed for his armchair.

"The teacher said."

"How can she sign it when she's—" he began. He sat down and fished the newspaper out of his briefcase.

I stood there staring at the newspaper, watched him bring his arms together to turn a page. Soon he'd ask me why I'm standing there.

"I'll sign it in the morning," he said finally.

When he handed it to me, just before I left for school, he didn't look up.

The day of the field trip we had to pack a lunch and bring money for milk. I was afraid to remind my father, but I had to. Why hadn't I told him sooner? he said. He put some salami between rye bread and gave me a quarter out of his pocket.

He looked at my jeans, about to speak. We're going to a farm, I told him.

The cows were milked in huge barns by machines with lots of metal and tubes. They explained all about it.

We had our lunch at picnic tables. They passed out little milk cartons with Hawthorn Mellody on the side. The milk tasted like grass.

We pulled out our sandwiches.

"What do you have?" asked Martha.

"Salami."

"That's funny," she said. "What's salami?"

I didn't know how to explain it.

"My mother always gives me cheese."

I almost said *Me, too,* because she did, and not on the rye bread my father gave me, which she knew I didn't like. But then Martha might ask why I didn't have cheese today.

Martha looked at my sandwich. I put it down on the bench where she couldn't see it. Later I threw it away.

"Is she coming home soon?" I asked my father when I dared.

"She'll come home when she's ready," he said.

⊗{ 8 }⊗

The bell rang, and we opened the front door and heard my father and Mel, Ginger's father, downstairs. Their voices mixed with the closed-in smell of the cool carpeted inner stairway, hardly used except for company and to get the mail, which the postman announced with two short rings, just before lunch.

From the landing we listened, Robbie and I, to shuffling sounds coming gradually closer, my father saying, "Just a little farther," and Mel's "That's good," slow and encouraging. We leaned over the railing, saw them turn at the first-floor landing to make the last two flights. My father supported her on one side, Mel on the other, with one hand under her arm and the other around her waist. She had on the dressing gown from England, the grey-blue check, dull-looking now. She was looking down, maybe to keep from catching the bottom of the bathrobe with her foot.

"One more step," my father said.

At the top, as she turned, I saw that the color had gone out of her. Her hair wasn't brown or blond but not another color either. It was wispy and short.

Was the cut under her bathrobe? If the robe opened,

could I see it? What had they taken out?

I backed through the door and into our front hallway, where they would pass again. She looked my way and started to speak, I thought, but then something seemed to grab her. She pulled the bathrobe closer, around her waist.

"Say hello to your mother," my father said.

She leaned heavier into Mel. They passed me just then.

"Why is she wearing a bathrobe?" I asked.

My father pulled her sudden and quick, away from me, and led her to their bedroom.

My father said we mustn't disturb her, so she could get better.

"I thought that's why she went away," I said. "To get better."

In the evening my father would open a can, Franco-American spaghetti or Chef Boyardee, and drop it in a pot and it came out a reddish mound on my plate. Sometimes the meatballs weren't heated all through, or the spaghetti. It was part hot, part cold, all in the same bite.

For his own supper he took out salami and Swiss cheese and Camembert, unwrapped the wax paper and made open sandwiches on hard dark pumpernickel. He waited till we were done—he didn't like to look at what we were eating. He didn't want us to watch him, either.

He heated up soup and poured it into a bowl and put

it on a tray, with some toast, and carried it down the hall and returned to the kitchen. He still didn't belong there, he still looked out of place.

He moved from their bedroom in front to the kitchen in back, bringing towels, glasses of water, toast he carried back untouched.

When she was strong enough she sat up, propped against pillows, and turned the pages of a magazine.

I brought a book and asked her to read it. She touched my hair and got that far-away look.

I pushed the book onto her lap.

She looked, opened it, started to read. She let me turn the pages.

A boy was taking a train journey, "all the way to Glasgow."

She told me that was in Scotland. We couldn't get there by train from here. But from London, where we came from, you could.

"Why is he going to Glasgow?" I asked.

We had to keep reading to find out. But after a few pages she was tired.

"We'll finish it later," she said. She shut her eyes.

Some days she got up and dressed in slacks and a sweater. They were big, hanging on her. Were they Daddy's, I wondered.

"No, mine," she answered, as if she wished they weren't.

She brushed her hair and put on lipstick. But when she saw herself in a mirror she put her hands to her face and turned away. She hung a coat over her bedroom-closet door, covering the mirror.

Some days my father took my mother back to the hospital, and when she came home she was sicker than before.

From the bathroom I heard terrible sounds. She half-leaned, half-slid along the hallway wall, dragging herself back to the bedroom.

She moved slowly, her limbs thinner, more difficult to move. It took everything she had to get from the stove to the table and sink into a chair.

"You've done too much," my father would say.

"Barely anything," she said.

These days ebbed, and if she got up it was only in her bathrobe, to lie down again.

We'd gone with my father to the hospital where he worked, one Saturday last year. He showed us his office, piled with papers, though not as many as at home. He led us down green-tiled halls, through oversized swinging doors, to the special room with the big equipment where he treated his patients. His—our!—name was stitched above the pocket of his white coat.

If I was sick, my father would take his penlight and look down my throat. He would press a cold stethoscope against my chest. He'd feel my swollen glands.

My father removed splinters with a needle from my mother's sewing kit, which he sterilized with a match. You had to hold very still. When it was out, he swabbed iodine, which burned.

He said my mother had "stomach troubles" and that she'd soon be better. To Leila he used the word "female." To Mr. Mandolasio, at the butcher's, he said, "Fine."

From the open door of the telephone closet, I thought I heard "impossible," but I couldn't be sure.

"It's his specialty," one day at Ginger's I heard Mel say to Leila. "Surely he knows."

We had to be careful. Not carry germs. Upset her with our movement, our noise. Interrupt her rest.

She needed rest, to get better.

If someone called our apartment, I hoped they wouldn't ask for her. Ask if she was there or could she come to the phone. I didn't like it when the phone rang.

The noise clanged out from the telephone closet, off the long hallway. The heavy black phone sat on old built-in drawers that had been painted over, so they didn't open, next to three or four big, dog-eared phone books. A light bulb with a pull-string hung over a canvas chair where we sat and poked at the plaster where it was gouged out, and we kept gouging it out, wider and wider. We could put our feet up against the drawers, which we weren't allowed to do anywhere else.

Still, I didn't want to talk on the phone at all. Usually it was for my parents or maybe my brother. They didn't really want me to answer. Only if no one else could.

If it was after school and Robbie was listening to music in his room or playing basketball over the closet door and the phone kept ringing, finally I would pick it up.

If I didn't say anything, they'd keep asking, "Are you there? Is anyone there?"

I knew I wasn't supposed to tell people. Not that I knew what to tell.

"Is anyone there?"

"You can't——" I'd say finally, and then if it was, say, one of their friends, like Lotte Feuerstein or Hilde Blaubender, they'd say, "Now, Julia——"

"You can't——" I'd say again. Even though I knew I wasn't supposed to say "You can't" to them.

If it was somebody else—because Lotte and Hilde knew, although they acted like they didn't——they might call right back, and the ringing would start all over again and seem louder and louder. If she was there, she wasn't supposed to be disturbed, so I had to answer it again.

When the phone rang I hoped it would stop before I got there to answer it. They didn't want to hear my voice anyway, they didn't want a six-year-old answering the phone. My brother was supposed to get it if my father wasn't home, but he might be out or in his room and not hear or pretend not to hear. My father wasn't home till three hours after school. But you can't just leave it ringing.

I wasn't supposed to answer the questions they were going to ask. *Where is she? How is she?* I didn't want to think about that either.

The girls stood all in a group in the corner of the playground, glancing sideways as I swayed on the swings, kicking my foot in the gravel.

I could see them whispering as we lined up to go back inside when the bell rang, whispering and giggling. I felt it on my skin.

They asked me questions I couldn't answer, that I knew I wasn't supposed to answer. Like the questions on the telephone. Rachel's mother had called, and Charlotte's.

I pulled my arms around me. I picked out stones in the gravel.

It was better when we were back in the classroom. Maybe they'd whisper but the teacher would make them stop.

After school I hoped Ginger wouldn't ask to come over.

My mother could be sitting there in her bathrobe, in the middle of the afternoon. She wouldn't even be reading, she wouldn't remember about milk and cookies.

"What's the matter with her?" Ginger could ask, even though she wasn't supposed to, I'd heard Leila tell her not to ask.

"Nothing," I'd say.

If I went to Ginger's house, I didn't have to think about it until my father came to pick me up—my father instead of my mother, not looking anyone in the face. Hurrying me off.

I would follow him up the front stairway and through the front door.

I mustn't say the wrong thing, ask the wrong questions. *What's wrong with her? When will she be better?*

Hadn't I learned yet not to ask? Didn't I know the harm that did? Hurting, hurting with my words, my noise. Not leaving her in peace.

I carried things in my head from school, the street, Ginger's, things that happened that perhaps I could describe and perhaps I couldn't.

Now if I brought my stories, my words disjointed perhaps, on what looked like a good day, trying to make a story, there was something that made me stop.

I sat at her feet, at the foot of the bed. At the foot of the bed of a sleeping person or a person not asleep but not awake either. Waiting for her to wake up, truly.

I tapped the covers at her feet to see if she was awake. She opened her eyes and seemed to smile.

"Come," she said, and I went a little closer. She spoke so quietly I could barely hear.

"Mommy," I'd begin, looking for words, words to give the picture I had in my mind.

"Tomorrow," she said. Her breath came in gasps. She drew her hand under the covers.

My words stuck in my mouth like stones. I wanted to spit them.

Why wasn't she fixed? Why was she more broken than before?

When my father called me to say goodnight I did not come. I sat cross-legged on the floor holding Milly and Silly. We swayed back and forth.

He came to the door. Didn't I hear him?

I stayed sitting, not looking up. I held onto my dolls.

I shook my head.

Take her back.

❦ 9 ❦

They took her back, Mel coming to help this time. He drove his car up in the front, double-parking, where Ginger and I were playing. "Watch it," he said. I'm going up."

We waited a long time, watching the car.

Leila opened the front door and held it while Mel and my father carried my mother out. She was on her feet but it was like they carried her, she looked small between them. Underneath her coat you could see the bathrobe and the bedroom slippers. I hoped Molly wouldn't come by just then.

"Open the door," Leila said, the car she meant. Ginger opened it. I stood back. I wanted to go round the corner.

They angled her onto the seat, and my father got in back. Mel drove. Leila went too.

In the playground Martha and Diane and Molly stood in a little circle, very close, and when I passed by they stopped talking and looked over. When we lined up to go inside at the bell they stared, and at recess when I walked up to Molly, she twisted her shoulder quick as could be and flung her head high and when she reached the others started to laugh.

At afternoon recess instead of running away they were looking for me, and when Molly came up she said, "They took her away again, didn't they?"

"Took who?"

"Your mom."

"So?"

"She won't be back this time."

"She will too."

"Not for long, my mom says."

"Not for long," echoed Diane.

"What does that mean?"

"Female stuff, my mom says." Molly knew everything

except what we learned in school.

"What's that?"

"The difference between boys and girls, silly," Molly said.

"Where the baby comes out," said Diane.

"What baby?"

"The baby, the one you're going to have."

"I'm not having any baby."

"Yeah, but your mother is."

"Not mine."

"Martha's then."

"Oh, that place."

"Between your legs."

"I've never seen it."

"You can't."

"Things fall out of it, then."

"The boy's thing goes in."

"I don't believe you."

"It's true."

"Is not."

"What else falls out?"

"Only babies."

"Are you sure?"

"Sure I'm sure."

"I don't believe it, anyway."

Maybe they took it out the hole. Robbie said they cut, but he could have been lying. It wouldn't be the first time.

It could have been a baby. But there wasn't any baby.

"My mom says she's not long for this world." That was Molly again.

"'Sick unto death,' my mom said. Those were her words. 'Ready for the priest she is,' my mom said."

"We don't have a priest," I told her. Though I wasn't sure what we did have.

"She meant ready to die. That's when you see the priest, silly."

"We don't have a priest," I said, as the bell rang.

My father arrived home later in the evenings, distracted, impatient.

"She's getting a rest now," he said after they had taken her back.

Were they cutting her open? Were they cutting her again?

"What rubbish," he said, his eyes narrowing. "They're taking care of her, and that's all."

"She's going to die, Molly said."

"You shouldn't listen to Molly."

"Molly's mother—"

"Mrs. McGwinn is an ignorant woman."

He turned and walked quickly down the hall.

When I went to my room he was sunk in the armchair, eyes closed, legs stretched and crossed, arm dropped to the floor, books and papers all over his lap.

If my mother opened the door, while I was holding my

dolls and trying to fall asleep, trying to wrap something around me, something I did not have, what would she look like? The edges were blurring, the center was falling away.

I learned to pick out my clothes, checking the patterns. But they didn't feel good, didn't feel like mine, were some other skin, uncomfortable, not fitting. They had lost their blessing.

⊛[10]⊛

When she came home she was even thinner than before, she had to be carried up the stairs. They had taken more out, then. She was more gone.

We had to be quiet and not disturb her. How could she get better if we didn't let her?

Still, sometimes I would stand by the door, even the closed door, because sometimes she came out. She had to come out sometime, didn't she?

I stood in the doorway and called her name, but she didn't answer.

If I went in there, surely she'd see me. Surely she'd speak.

I crept in toward the bed. She was facing away from me. I had to call her name again, louder.

"Mommy."

Why didn't she talk? Why didn't she answer?

I had my speller in my hand, and my spelling homework. She liked to help me with it.

If only she'd turn her head, then she'd see me. Wouldn't she answer if she knew?

"Mommy!"

Now she started to turn but if she saw me she didn't smile or say anything. My father looked like that when I did something, or Robbie did, and he was going to box our ears. She turned away again.

I stretched out my arms to put the book and the spelling sheet next to the pillow, so she'd see. But she didn't. She didn't turn around.

"What are you doing?" I heard my father say. He came up behind me. He grabbed my arm and pulled me back.

The book flew out of my hands. It hit the doorpost and split in two.

He took the speller, the pages that were in two parts, and held it in front of my face.

"See what you've done. See what you've done already," he said.

I'd see what happens if I don't leave her in peace.

My father was a doctor, he ought to know.

He'd like to break me in two like the book, my father said, he'd like to break something in two.

I would too. If I had a knife big enough I'd help him.

In my room I picked up Rosemary. She was thin, my hand could almost go around her waist. Her dress was silky, like a grownup dress, snug to the hips, a going-out dress.

Rosemary's lips, sculpted and red, curved upward. Her eyes, under feathery lashes, opened when I held her up straight. They were blue like my mother's. They stared, empty and blank.

Rosemary was hard, her molded body and her stiff cold limbs. She flew out of my hands, I could hear her crash across the room.

I found Rosemary in the corner. She had hit the bookcase, the back of her head cracked open. A piece of scalp, with the strands of hair sprouting from tiny, perfect holes, flapped from behind her ear. Her skull had split, showing the hollow inside. Her eyes still stared, her lips still smiled.

I picked up Rosemary and flung her down the length of my closet, way to the end where no one would find her.

Look at those curls, people used to say, running an uninvited hand over my hair. Don't you look like your mother? Her hair had been fair, too, when she was young.

I was curled around myself, I was joined to her, we were one person. Like hard-folded petals, one around the other.

The poison in her in me too.

How could it be otherwise?

So it was poison.

Did I carry in the germs on the soles of my improperly wiped boots, under my fingernails, in my nose, needing a handkerchief, my throat, congested?

My father would shine his flashlight in my throat. At least he didn't put a stick down there, like Dr. Baensch. "A little pink," he'd say, withdrawing the light. "Where do you keep getting these things?" But it was my mother, not him, who'd crushed the aspirin on a spoon and mixed it with orange juice and told me it wasn't so bad.

Wash your hands before dinner. After touching money. When you come inside. Don't take a sip of his drink. Hands out of your hair. Your nose. Your mouth.

Careful when you wipe, wash your hands afterward, did you wash your hands?

Maybe germs could get in there too. They had gotten into her maybe that way even though I didn't see how. Or maybe in a drink like in Robbie's comic or from the handkerchief that my father was always telling me to pick up off the table, it was full of germs. I'd make everyone sick, didn't I care? Wasn't one sick person in the house enough?

It worked from the inside out, eating away, I could see that, even though my father said it was a lie, a terrible cruel lie, how could I wish something like that on my mother? I could see it, almost, the stuff inside collapsing.

The female stuff, whatever that was. I stayed in the bathroom patting myself, holding it together. How could anything get in, or come out? I closed my legs, keeping it safe. What was *it*?

She tread cautiously, almost transparent, her but not her.

She paused to steady herself on the way to or from the bathroom, holding the doorframe, leaning against the wall.

She looked at me, frightened. She said my name and stepped, faltering, on her way.

I felt dizzy. I got a sick taste in my mouth, like I was going to throw up.

If I threw up wouldn't he say, "One sick person in the house is enough"? And I would say, "You said she was getting better," and he would say, "How dare you." So I kept it down, carried it with me, just under my tongue. It rose inside my mouth. I forced it down again.

She was fine, my father said, only tired, she'd be better next week.

"When is that?"

She'll get well, my father said, if you let her.

Did I look like my mother now, with her skin which had been so smooth, so full of light, now falling into little ashy pieces?

◈⊰ 11 ⊱◈

They came with an ambulance, which spun its lights but no siren. It double-parked on Magnolia, under the heavy drooping trees, the bright red flashing. I looked out my window, over the desk. My father had said, "Stay there, keep out of the way."

Footsteps and voices in the foyer. I cracked my door and saw two men cross and enter their bedroom carrying long poles between them. Voices from there, bumping sounds. They carried her out like an Indian, strapped, holding the poles. Indians carried their babies like that.

"Be careful," my father said to the men. "For God's sake be careful, can't you see—"

I heard voices on the stairs as they went down. They must have had to tip those poles a lot. My father kept telling them to be careful.

I lost the sound as they got to the bottom, and went back to the window.

They laid her on the grass just like the furniture when we moved. My father was gesticulating. One of them went behind the ambulance and opened the doors and then they came back and picked up the stretcher and maneuvered it inside.

It was hard to see through the trees and the car that was parked by the curb, blocking my view.

The driver motioned to my father to get in the back, but he didn't. At last he got in on the passenger side, and the other man went in back. The door closed and they pulled away. Now they started the siren.

In my closet I turned Rosemary over so I couldn't see the wound and tucked a skirt around her like a blanket.

Sometimes I crept into the closet, which was narrow and dark and long, picked up Rosemary and smoothed the skirt, felt the wound, told her I was sorry, sorry. Told her she had to get well.

I found my own clothes and dressed myself and threaded the barrette into my hair as best I could. If I came home after school instead of Ginger's, I sat alone at the dining-room table doing my sums, copying my spelling. When I finished I wanted to tear it up.

My father began to put the house in order.

Robbie's schoolwork had been scuttled, unfinished, on the sideboard. No wonder his grades were so poor, my father said, thrusting the papers into Robbie's reluctant hands. The teacher would be fully in her rights to fail him.

In their bedroom dishes lay uncollected.

Articles of clothing had been dropped in odd places: Robbie's baseball cap under the dining room table, a cardigan of my mother's draped over the back of the canvas chair in the telephone closet. Who had she called?

My jacket he found in the pantry, where I must have let it fall while searching for cookies after school.

When he picked me up from Ginger's he was not more silent; he had been silent before. But he was more set in his silence.

My brother would come over from his friend Douglas's at six and wait on the steps for my father. He didn't want to come in, where Ginger and I were, girls, babies, and only entered if Leila insisted.

My father no longer said thank you to Leila when he arrived with the newspaper under his arm and the briefcase in his hand after the day. Stepping into a house with the smells of dinner, the settling of evening, private and closed. Mel home, padding down the stairs in his comfortable shoes, as if, gracious as he was, greeting, asking about Eve, he had been holding himself until he heard my father at the door and knew the children were now going to be cleared, taken home. The children not his. Leila perhaps didn't mind but for Mel it was strange, as strange as for my father.

In the evening Robbie would tell my father about his baseball game and maybe the Cubs score if he had heard it on the radio. Sometimes while he was sitting on their steps Mel would pass by the screen door and tell him that the Cubs won or lost, or were hanging on in the ninth.

My father had read the box scores of yesterday's game in the newspaper, kept the averages in his head.

"Two more wins and they'll be playing five hundred,"

he said to my brother as we walked home.

"They're lousy against the Pirates."

"Of course the season is young."

"Can we go Saturday?" my brother asked.

The summer before my father had taken both of us, packing sandwiches in a bag that we carried on the El and Robbie was too embarrassed to eat.

"Hot dogs, Dad. People eat hot dogs at the ball game."

We took the El south from Thorndale and changed at Belmont for the train that stopped at Addison. There were "A" trains and "B" trains, which stopped at alternate stations.

People got on along the way, and you could tell they were going to the ballpark—mothers carrying cooler bags and boys in T-shirts and baseball caps talking loud together.

We sat in the bleachers, the only tickets left. We climbed so many steps to get there and then where we sat was like steps too. Robbie said it was the place to be, unless you could sit on the first base line, of course, like Joey's dad.

The Cubs were losing. Men drinking beer next to us yelled Polish curses. They brought their lunch too, thick sausages wrapped in heavy pieces of bread.

My father wouldn't buy Robbie a hot dog, we had brought our own food. Around the sixth inning Robbie stuck his hand inside the bag and pulled off a piece of sandwich and popped it in his mouth.

"What're you staring at?" he said when he caught me looking at him.

He kept sneaking bites until he'd probably eaten a whole sandwich. Then he was thirsty. He asked my father to get him a Coke.

"The game's almost over."

"It's only the seventh. I'm thirsty."

When one of the barkers came by with his tray of Cokes my father asked how much they were and started to shake his head when he heard the answer, but Robbie said "Come on!" and he got the Coke, which we shared.

When the sun grew long and deep into the bleachers my father suddenly said, "Why don't we get some peanuts," and then he showed us how to squeeze open the shells and slide off the inner skin before we ate them. "The shells are poison, you know," he told us.

The crowd started heading out in the top of the eighth but my father wanted to stay. The probability of a turn-around isn't high, he said, but it's not impossible. By the time it was over they'd lost eight to two, and it was a long sad line getting into the Addison Street station.

He took us again, just before school started, and this time we didn't bring our lunch. When the man came by shouting "Hot dogs, hot dogs, get yer red hots here!" my father waved and the man brought them over and my father bought three, one for each of us, and asked for mustard on his.

Robbie was happy. The Cubs pulled it out in the ninth, two to one.

But this year if we wanted to go, the answer was always No.

❧ 12 ❧

On Mother's Day my father went out early and came back with flowers wrapped in paper.

"We're going to see her," Robbie said. "And you're not."

It wasn't fair. Why could Robbie go and I couldn't?

"He's older," said my father.

"I have something to give her!"

"Give it here."

At school Mrs. Dermott had said, "Ask your mother for recipes and we'll copy them onto cards and illustrate them and make a pretty cover and punch holes and tie ribbon through it and you'll all have presents for Mother's Day. Three recipes, not too difficult or long."

"She won't know," Mrs. Dermott said to Diane, who didn't want to give the surprise away. "Tell her we're learning about food."

"Recipes for what?"

"Her favorites—ask what her favorites are."

I had watched her make the potato things, the ingredients floating into the bowl, coming up mixed out of her hands. I didn't remember what they were called.

Where could I find recipes? I didn't know if they were in her head or on paper, or in a book like the teacher said was okay if your mother didn't have her own (only it clearly wasn't as good). I could picture her with a book open on the kitchen table, lots of books, but wasn't she reading a story?

Where did she keep them?

In the pantry maybe, within the piles of papers and mail, or in the heavy drawers I couldn't open. I didn't see a box marked "Recipes" like Mrs. Dermott said some mothers have, our presents will fit right in those boxes.

In the corner next to the breadbox were some falling-apart books with faded titles, like some of the books on my father's shelf that were in German. Way to the right was something newer, a big thick book I pulled out and opened. It wasn't covered in type like the ones my mother liked to read but had numbers along with words and lists, something like a speller. These were recipes, but so many of them, with so many words I didn't know.

How did I know what her favorites were?

Cakes she liked, didn't she, so I stopped there, so many cakes, we only needed three. I pulled three pages out of the book.

"Your mother gave you these?" said Mrs. Dermott, leaning over my desk.

There were so many words, I saw now, trying to copy them over, I could never fit them on a card.

"How did these pages get pulled out of a book?" She picked up the sheets, turned them over. "Out of a book? Torn from a book?"

Her voice was rising, kids were turning around. Molly looked over knowingly.

"What did we learn, class," Mrs. Dermott asked, "about taking care of books? Do you remember?"

I couldn't answer, couldn't look her in the face.

Molly leaned over and whispered to Diane, and they both giggled. I thought I heard "her mother." Mrs. Dermott turned that way.

I looked down at the gouged-out initials on the top of my desk, the white fists of my hands, the hard-worn strips of the wooden floor, seamed unevenly, like the longest thinnest stairsteps. I felt tears rising in my eyes. I wanted to disappear inside my desk. I waited and waited.

Mrs. Dermott stepped toward Molly's desk, and Molly and Diane stopped whispering. Mrs. Dermott, as if hearing or remembering, got a new look on her face.

Then, as suddenly as she had started, Mrs. Dermott put the papers down and changed her voice, softened, quieted. She knelt next to me and turned the pages again, slowly, picked up my pencil from the desk and marked off three places, saying, "Here, I think these will be easiest, just write this part, don't worry."

Mrs. Dermott punched holes in the cards, passed out construction paper for the book cover, and gave us ribbon to tie it with.

My father and Robbie forgot to take the recipe book.

They left carrying the flowers, a smirk on Robbie's face, but they came back silent.

I stuck the booklet into the pocket of a dress on a hanger in her closet, not the blue one, the pockets weren't big enough, and it didn't belong there, she wouldn't wear it to cook in. In the sundress with yellow flowers, delicate and star-shaped, swirling up diagonally, dancing. It had yellow buttons that were much brighter than the flowers now, after being washed so many times, and big patch pockets where she was always putting things, and forgetting them. She'd be reading me a story and reach in and pull out a postcard from her brother Lewis, a photo of Buckingham Palace on the back, laughing, "Oh, I wondered where this went to. I really owe him an answer!"

So the next time she would put it on, which would be soon, it was warm now, she'd feel something in the pocket and reach in, and out would come the recipe book and she would say "Oh, what's this?" never having seen it before, that would be different, not something she stuck there herself. "What's this?" she would say and touch the ribbon and see the writing on the front, *My Favorite Recipes*, the letters crunching over to the right where I ran out of room, and open it up and smile. "Where did this come from?" she'd say, with a joke in her voice, and I'd say, "I don't know," joking too. Then she'd bend down and hug me. Wouldn't she?

⊛{ 13 }⊛

For her birthday my father bought my mother a suitcase.

"We'll bend the rules just this once," my father said. His or the hospital's? He didn't say. They'd take me with them today. Leila came too.

The nurses exchanged puzzled looks when we passed their desk, my father with the suitcase in his hand.

"You wait here," my father said, as he went in. Leila stood with me at the doorway. Robbie slid inside the room and leaned against the wall.

My father laid the suitcase on the bed.

"Now we'll go on holiday," he told her.

Unlatching the lever under the bed with his foot, he let down the railing. It lowered like a crib but the bars ran sideways instead of up and down and they were metal, not wood. Through the slats I could see a ridge in the covers. He lifted the suitcase and placed it on the blanket next to the ridge. It was navy with a cord of white around the edge, matching her spring dress, he said. A red ribbon was tied around it.

An upside-down bottle hung on a stand like a coat-rack, with a tube leading under the bedclothes. Except for the suitcase, everything was white.

My father undid the ribbon and unsnapped the clasps, opened the top, ran his hand along the deep-blue lining, drew back the pockets. He pulled some shiny papers out of the long pocket in back, travel brochures, which he un-folded and lined up on the tray in front of her.

If she had been able to raise her head, she would have seen them: glossy photographs of the Rocky Mountains, snow-covered, skirted with wildflowers. The main lodge and cabins where we were going to go last summer. The Denver Zephyr, silvery, snaking alongside a river.

I couldn't see her face or even if it was her.

My father kept speaking to the bed, the pillow, from which some thin slate-colored hair stuck out.

"It's what you wanted, remember? Going away, you said. A journey. Here, we'll do it together, it's all arranged. I only need to get the tickets, as soon as you're out—"

He shifted the booklets on the tray, turned them over so the photographs changed.

"We'll get a cabin, with a bath." He pointed to a pic-ture. "Near the lodge."

As he sat down on a chair next to the bed, his hands went up, clutched his temples, covered his face. There was no movement from the bed, no sound anywhere.

Robbie edged closer to the door.

Leila pushed her palm against my back. "Go ahead."

She slipped into my hand a little package covered with colored paper and tied with a white cloth ribbon. "Give this to your mother."

I took two steps and saw through the slats on the pillow a face, grey and gone, an old woman whom I did not know.

No wonder she didn't answer. Didn't they realize?

A hand stuck out of the slats.

"Give her the present," Leila said. I felt my breath catch in my throat. My throat swelled, shutting off the air.

My father didn't look up.

Without air, I could not speak.

"Go ahead."

I stepped again and reached to put the box in the hand, which could barely get fingers around it.

"Thank you, Julia," I thought I heard. The voice was shaky yet somehow familiar.

I looked toward the bed, the eyes opened a little.

Leila came over and lifted the box out of her hand before it dropped.

She took Robbie and me home on the El, leading us silently at first, then talking too much, unable to stop talking.

I held Milly in one arm and Silly in the other. They were round and padded baby dolls and nestled in the crook of my arms.

"Have you been good girls?" I asked them, and each nodded in her turn.

"Really good?" They promised they had.

"Well, if you've been very good, we can go and visit. But you must be very very good and very very quiet."

They promised they would be.

"Just for a minute. She needs to rest."

We went into the closet, crouching down, tiptoeing.

"Ssshhh," I said.

When we got to the back we sat down where Rosemary lay in her skirt-bed on the floor. I picked up the skirt and she turned over. It showed her head cracked open, the hair splayed in two directions, half of her skull flapped aside.

Ooohhhh, Milly said, real long and slow.

"SSShhhhh!"

What happened to her? Milly wanted to know.

"Nothing," I said. "Nothing."

Yes it did.

"Don't say that, Milly," I said. "Watch out—"

It did, it did.

"You can't say that."

Milly started shaking then, shaking in my hand, and then she hit Rosemary and sent her scudding farther into the closet. *Go away*, she said.

"Stop it, Milly," I said, quietly, then louder. "You can't talk like that."

She's gone, Milly said. *She left.*

"She didn't leave, you threw her."

I don't care.

"You promised to be good. If you're not careful—"

I don't care, Milly said.

"You can't say that," I said. "You'll have to be punished."

I put her down and got my chair and dragged it into

the hall, got up and pulled down my mother's sewing kit from the shelf in the closet. I took out her scissors. They weren't as sharp as my father's, but she wouldn't mind my using them, the way he did.

I took the tip of the scissors and pierced her, right in the stomach. The scissors went in easier than I thought, she was soft there. They made an ugly jagged hole.

"You have to learn," I said.

Then I held them both, Milly and Silly, and rocked and rocked. After a long time I looked at Milly, at what I had done, and I held her against me and ran down to the kitchen and threw her in the garbage.

It was in Ginger's kitchen that my brother told me our mother had died.

"I don't believe you," I said. He was always lording it over me.

"It's true, though," he said, his voice dull and uninflected. He might have told me it had started to rain.

I went into the living room and stared at the fireplace, the irregular surface of the fieldstones, with their shades of black and grey and slate-blue, set one next to the other, from the hearth to the mantel above my head.

I examined the peaks and valleys of the stones. I ran my eye across, then down, then across again the other way. Between the stones ran muddy ribbons of cement. My eye could travel along them forever. How hard the stones were, and how sculpted, as if by water, and how perfectly they fit together.

III
The Empty Quarter

❦ 14 ❧

They went, my father in dark wool on the hot June day, Robbie in a suit that stopped at his ankles.

Who stayed with me I do not remember. Maybe it was Leila's sister, the frowsy Iris, in her shapeless collared dresses with the uneven hems and lace-up oxfords. Difficult to imagine these two as sisters—Iris, looking like a grandmother, and Leila, her blond hair stylishly brushed up in little waves, her blue eyes sparkling, and always dressed for lunch downtown. High-spirited Leila, who got the looks in the family.

Leila and Iris would have decided between them how things should be arranged. "And Julia," Leila would have said, slowly, quietly, as if imparting a secret, "of course Julia is too young to go," and Iris would have clicked her tongue and nodded into the phone. And so they would have taken my grief into their hands, and out of mine. Just as Leila would tell our neighbors, and the mothers of my friends, her bridge partners and Mrs. Davidson at the bakery that my mother had "passed away."

But if Iris had come all the way from the suburb where she lived, she would have gone to the funeral herself, so she couldn't have been the one who stayed with me. She would have placed herself prominently among the mourners, next to her sister, who belonged there. She would have puffed herself up in an ill-fitting black dress, her indignant shoulders passing their own judgment on the unnatural event.

Maybe it was Mrs. Ewen or a babysitter hired for the occasion, an elderly widow from an agency, or a recipient of Leila's charity work at a center for the poor. She would have sat herself in the living room, in my father's armchair, reading a magazine or bent over knitting needles clacking away.

In my room the emptiness pressed against me, and outside my window the catalpa leaves luffed in the sweet June breeze. The apartment was silent, emptied of her, emptied of what held it together.

The doorbell rang and they came one after another, the people with accents who used to come for dinner, and neighbors, and doctors and their wives. A few, knowing the Jewish custom, came the back way, so as not to ring the bell. Leila had left the door ajar.

They entered with muffled voices as if afraid of waking someone, as if still she was sleeping or not sleeping in the bedroom. They brought food in dishes covered with foil or wax paper or yet another dish, big heavy bowls still warm, baskets of fruit, bakery boxes tied with string.

The Feuersteins stepped into the hallway and spoke in long hushed sentences. The Blaubenders in their finery came to the back door, a large oval casserole in Hilde's plump hands. She carried it to the kitchen where Leila was organizing the offerings. Dorothea Stern insisted on going back to help.

People came who did not fit, whom I had never seen in our apartment before. The Mandolasios, who owned the butcher's and lived three houses away, and the Larsens, our downstairs neighbors, who gestured apologetically from the door and weren't sure they ought to come inside. Mrs. McGwinn, Molly's mother, appeared at the front, carrying a bottle of wine.

Each one came quietly but together they made noise. As they forgot their quietness they spoke a babble of tongues. The gutteral voices of the Feuersteins and the Blaubenders mixed in with those of the Mandolasios and the Ewens and Mrs. McGwinn, and Leila and Mel, and sounded off-key. What were they doing here together?

The colors blurred as one put an arm around the shoulder of another, they touched cheeks, spoke words like "tragedy" and "mercy" and "cut short." They formed and unformed circles, showing their backs.

My father sat on the piano bench brought from the sunroom. Mel said my father ought to sit on a hard bench.

They went to my father, leaned down speaking in low tones, left room for his reply, and after a time moved on, taking food on a plate and talking about other things.

They did not see me under the piano, holding Silly in my arms. My father did not turn around, he'd have told me to come out of there, it was dirty. Leila had cleaned everything that morning, but he'd say it anyway. Leila came early and pulled the broom and the vacuum out from the back porch and pushed them into corners and dusted the tops of things. "How long hasn't this been done?" she said, shaking her head. "There will be people coming tonight. You have to be ready."

We watched through the silk tassels of the piano skirt dripping nearly to the floor. I told Silly we were safe there. The big people were not interested, would not look for us. They were passing something from one to the other, I explained to her. Could she see it, when their shoulders met and their arms circled each other? The way they held together for moments, close? They passed it all around, adding something each time.

"Do you remember when Mommy used to pass us things, and we passed them back?" I asked her. I barely could.

What kinds of things, Silly wanted to know.

"Things you can't see," I told her. "Anyway, they're gone now."

In her closet garments remained in an orderly row, draped over their hangers: the drab wools of London; the dresses she wore when company came, her "one dress," actually two, some air of festivity and peril clinging to them still; the cotton housedresses of hot Chicago summers, softened by wear, by resting on her skin. I ran my hand along the skirts, puffing them out. I lifted them one by one, making motion and air, making them dance. They cooled me like a fan.

The full skirt of the new blue dress puffed out on its own. It didn't need me to help it.

I couldn't lift the hanger off the pole so I pulled the dress off the hanger. I rolled it up, tucked it under Silly, and stepped across the hall to my room.

"Here, Silly," I said, dropping her onto the bed. "You wait here."

The scissors were in the sewing box, no one had touched them. I carried them back to my room, into the closet, with the dress. My first cuts were lightning but then they slowed in the big expanse of cloth. I let go the scissors and grabbed the material in my hands, pulled it apart, hearing the rushing-hard rip, even better than the sound of the cutting. I tore off the strips and dropped them on the floor, next to Rosemary.

I started in the middle, winding the cloth. I wrapped the first strip around, slowly. I lifted her up and turned the cloth over and patted it against her and then put her down, on my legs, and smoothed it out, and said, "There." Each piece I wrapped a little higher, covering her bit by bit. I wound a strip around and around her head, over the top and under her chin, like a hood, binding her wound. Then I worked back down around the arms and along the legs. Her arms and legs couldn't move but it didn't matter now. Her face still smiled, looked calm. I didn't cover her face. I believed the calm now.

I brought her out and put her on the bed, next to Silly. I took a shoebox from the shelf and took out the paper dolls that were inside and carried the shoebox over to the bed. I lifted Rosemary into the box and covered it and put it under the bed, pushing it as far back as I could, into the corner.

I picked up Silly and held her tight.

❧ 15 ❧

At the end of the week my father said it was time, I was going back to school.

I was awake under the tent of my sheet. The heat had come up, a hot desert wind filling my room.

They had special hot winds in the desert that blew for days, heavy and thick. We'd seen a film in school about the Bedouin of Arabia, who traveled in caravans along the edge of the Empty Quarter, the largest sand desert on Earth. It showed nomads riding camels, sitting in tents, squatting by open fires, children playing with pieces of cloth and hunks of rock, drawing their games with a stick in the sand. They wrapped themselves in cool white clothing and searched for oases.

When the winds came up the nomads stayed in their tents, and if they had to go out they covered their faces. The sands blowing made it dark as night. You couldn't tell front from back, up from down.

The winds brought illnesses. Tiny particles of sand

invaded the lungs, causing choking and suffocation—suffocation in open air. The nomads sought shelter, and even in shelter did not always find safety.

I had pulled the sheet over my head. "It's the wind," I told my father. "I'm safe in the tent."

"Nonsense," he said. "It's time to get up."

"No air." The air was gone, sucked out by the wind, the oppressive heat.

Hadn't they complained about it, returning from the cemetery, sweaty and glassy-eyed?

"Of course there's no air under the sheet," he said. "Come out now. Stop this nonsense."

"I can't breathe."

I put the sheet over my face, and it was hard to breathe. He grabbed it and pulled it off.

"This is why you can't breathe—"

"I still can't."

I couldn't breathe, he just couldn't see it.

He made me go.

"Who will stay home with you?"

I stepped between the desks keeping my eyes on the floor, slipping into my seat, ducking my head, looking for my books.

Mrs. Dermott was careful not to call on me, went along every row but mine, skipped our reading group, saying there wasn't time.

At the recess bell I followed at the end of the file of kids, hanging back, waiting for the games to start. But the girls just stood there, poking toes in the gravel.

"Where were you, Julia?" Martha said, after a silence.

"Nowhere."

"I saw you yesterday, you weren't sick," said Diane.

"So."

"Your mom died, my mother said so," said Molly.

"She did not."

"She did too. My mom was there."

"She saw it?" asked Diane.

"Saw her die?"

"After," said Molly.

"My grandfather died, he went for a long sleep, my mom said. We can't see him now," said Harriet.

"So," said Betsy.

"My brother's dog got run over, and they got him another one," said Martha.

"The first one was so cute," said Betsy.

"This one is okay," said Martha. "He's stopped barking."

"Okay," Ginger finally said. "What are we going to play?"

When school got out we went to the beach again. Leila would take us, driving her car the few blocks we used to walk carrying all our gear. She'd smear lotion on her body, set up a huge umbrella high on the beach, and stay out of the sun.

Ginger and I took pails and shovels down to the water, where the sand became cool.

I had brought Rosemary in my bucket, where Leila couldn't see her, and set the bucket on the sand a little higher, before the wet part. Ginger helped me dig. We each used a shovel, watching the dry sand slide in and shoveling it out again. I thought it should be an up-and-down hole but Ginger said sideways, that's how they bury people. So we spread it out some more, working against the sand that kept slipping back in.

"Now," she said, and I laid Rosemary in it, but it still wasn't deep enough.

We dug down and out along a line, eventually hit the damp sand.

"This is far enough," I said. I didn't want her to get wet.

I laid Rosemary in the hole, then lifted her to make sure the dampness hadn't seeped onto the cloth that was wrapped around her.

"It's okay, I guess."

I put her back in and we covered her over.

I waded into the water up to my waist, then plunged under, not noticing the cold. I paddled a little, put my feet down, paddled some more. The wind was blowing the water sideways, an extra line of waves.

I wished I could swim.

I returned to my mother's closet, carrying Silly, forgetting why.

I fanned the skirts of her dresses, heard the rustling. I pulled the recipe book out of the pocket of the yellow-flowered dress.

"Oh," I said, the way she'd say it, "what's this?"

We took the booklet back to my room and sat down on the bed. I held Silly in my arms and turned the pages. "Applesauce Cake," "Apple Spice Cake," "Banana Orange Cake."

I pulled at the bow, gently, not to let it untie.

She wasn't going to find it now.

It burned my fingers. I wanted to scratch my own skin.

I opened the bottom drawer of my desk, where I kept birthday cards and the few letters I'd gotten, and postcards my father sent when he went to meetings. I put it under the letters, for safekeeping.

"Silly," I said, "what do we do now?"

I carried Silly everywhere, even though Robbie made fun of me.

"Look at the baby," he'd say.

I gave her bits of my dinner until my father said she couldn't come to the table. She wasn't alive.

I brought the pieces to her, hiding them in my pockets and removing them far back in the safety of my closet. They collected on the floor there, drying out, growing mold.

"Silly, you haven't been eating," I told her one day. "Naughty girl." I put them on a paper and threw them away. "It's wasteful, you know."

I read her my homework, my spelling words. She learned how to give them back. It was tutoring now, no longer a class.

I stood on a chair and wedged *Bartholomew and the Oobleck* behind the top row of the bookshelf, where I wouldn't be able to see it. When Ginger asked about it, I told her it was lost. At her house she read *Horton Hatches the Egg*, which reminded me too. I told her I was sick of it.

Luckily the teacher didn't read those books to us any more. Now we could read ourselves.

IV
Pangaea

⊗〔 16 〕⊗

When Dora came she took my mother's clothes out of the closet and packed them in a carton from Kroger's that said Clorox in big letters on the side.

I wasn't supposed to say "my mother" that way and didn't say it and never would say it again. Leila told us to call Dora that and so we did, though it stuck in my throat and I had to have something crossed, like my fingers behind my back, at least I meant them to be.

I watched her. I watched as she went into the closet, which was in the back right-hand corner of their bedroom, past the double bed, which took up most of the room, and the high dark-wood dresser. She reached in and pulled them out, not one by one, but in a bunch as big as she could carry in her arms. I saw the housecoat with the little pink flowers, the yellow sundress, a brown nubby wool that came from England. There were the blue jeans from Colorado, when we went to visit my grandparents, and the pale-blue dress with the velvet sash she put on, adjusting the bow, when people came over. Dora tossed them on the bed.

I watched as she loaded them up and flung them down. Dora was lean, with honey-blond hair waved carefully behind the ears. She dressed in tailored, creased pants and sharply pressed blouses.

I didn't stop her. I let Dora take the clothes out of the

closet, the dresses my mother had worn. They had been washed a hundred times, until the colors faded and the cloth wore thin.

Dora opened a box and took each dress off its hanger and laid it neatly on the bed and folded it, two sides to the middle and then in thirds, and put it in the box. She cleared the top of the dresser with the lacquered box where my mother kept her jewelry and her few perfumes with their scalloped glass plugs. The lace doily had collected so much dust, Dora said as she shook it out, away from herself, couldn't anyone see how perfectly useless it was. She picked up each piece and wrapped it in newspaper and put it in the carton. She pulled open the drawers and took out piles of my mother's underwear and slips and nightgowns, the silk one patterned in Oriental blossoms she packed in the train case and the flannels she wore even in the spring, when she could not feel the warmth, when she was shivering.

The dresses mocked me, they had turned away. I was glad Dora was packing them. I never wanted to see them again.

No air inside now, just blackness, the dresses flattened like dead leaves in the fall. My father carried the box to the back porch. It was freezing out there, with only screens, the winter came right up over the wooden porch slats. He couldn't find tape so he folded over the flaps and placed a tennis racket in a heavy wooden press on top of the box, to keep it closed.

Leila had taken me to Marshall Field's to buy me a dress.

"No," I said.

"We'll find you something very pretty," she said.

"I don't want to."

"Don't you want to look pretty?"

"What do you mean?"

"Well, it's a wedding, people get dressed up."

She took my hand up the escalator to the fifth floor, pushed the dresses along the rack and asked me what size I wore, but I didn't know. She pulled one out and held it against me. A saleslady came up shaking her head.

"That will never fit," she said. She went down the rack and found the same dress, twice as big, bulky. She pulled out some others, slung them over her arm and carried them into a fitting room ahead of us.

In the mirror I saw a giant, taller than everyone in my class, chunky and round. There were mirrors on three sides, reflecting myself back, over and over.

Leila lifted a dress off its hanger. I stuck my arms through the sleeves and pulled the dress down, then she zipped it up. I had to inhale. It pinched at the back and stretched against my waist.

Finally one fit, a dark-red taffeta, below the knee. A trim of little loops circled near the bottom of the skirt and around the yoke. It had puffed sleeves, a little tight around my arms, but it didn't pull too much around the middle.

"Isn't that beautiful?" Leila said. I had never had anything like this, silky and long, a deep, grown-up color. But my pale pudgy arms gave everything away.

"It's stupid," I said.

Leila insisted, had me take it off and gave it to the saleslady to wrap. Then she found me some patent-leather shoes with bows on the front.

"Now, aren't you glad you came along?" Leila said as we got off the El train at Thorndale station.

"I'll be wearing black," Leila had said, on the phone, maybe to her sister, I'd overheard it.

Her dress turned out to be black and white, alternating swatches angling across, black and white shoes, bag too.

"She looks like a clown," whispered Ginger, tugging at the lacy neckline of her pink velvet dress. She hated dresses, had to wear them to school but that was the limit.

My brother had a new suit, too big instead of too small. The collar stood out a mile in back.

They found a rabbi, maybe the one who gave the eulogy. Cut down in her prime, he would have said, the young life snuffed out.

Now, under the *chuppa*, "Do you?" he solemnly asked. Yes, yes, they do. "Till death do us part."

Dora's aqua scoop-necked dress, full-skirted almost to

the ankles, shimmered a little, caught the light. My father wore his pin-striped wool suit. It must have been hot in June, just right for December. He crushed the glass under old black wing-tips that had a hole working its way into the bottom.

Ginger rated the dresses and jewelry on the ladies and noticed whether the men could dance.

Our across-the-hall neighbors, the Ewens, sat solitary at one end of the table. My father's colleagues from the hospital talked busily at the other.

Dorothea Stern came over to where Ginger and I were sitting.

"Hello, my dear," she said, too sweetly, touching me on the head, which I hated. "Isn't this lovely?"

I made some sound, not words.

"Now you have a new mother, isn't that wonderful." It wasn't a question.

"Dora," she said. "A new mother, we're so happy for you, Kurt and I--everyone."

Dora took everything out of the pantry, filled a pail with soapy water, and with an old shirt of my father's scrubbed down the shelves and wiped the cabinets clean. She pulled out the drawers and dumped their crumbs and washed and dried them before putting them back. She emptied the refrigerator and washed it out and then the landlord brought a new one.

More boxes got packed up. Dora found my mother's coat with the fox collar in the hall closet along with several pairs of galoshes I'd outgrown and a snowsuit from when I was five. My father's raincoat, in there too, had a big rip running up the side where he'd snagged it getting off the El.

She marked neatly with a pen on each carton which room it came from, and the cartons were piled up on the porch.

My father missed his raincoat, he'd bought it in London, saved ration points for months and months. A proper British waterproof was one thing you couldn't find in America.

Dora came into my room asking, "What's her name?" I was reading Silly a book which was open on the floor.

Dora sat on the bed and crossed her legs. She smoothed out the top of her slacks, ran her fingertip along the crease, which stood up like the edge of a paper. Her hand traced the line.

I didn't answer so she asked again.

"Elizabeth," I told her.

"Such a nice name," she said. I could hear her accent, on the "such" especially. One hand covered the other, on her knee.

"You have other dolls?"

I shook my head. I held Silly and turned the page,

even though we hadn't read it.

"I used to have dolls," she said. "They were beautifully made, with perfect little porcelain faces. They had the most exquisite dresses, which my grandmother made."

Dora crossed her legs the other way and pinched the crease on the new top leg, making it straight.

"I can crochet a dress for Elizabeth, just like I used to have," she said. "If you let me see her, I'll know what size to make it."

I picked up Silly from the floor and held her in my lap. I smoothed down her hair.

"She has a dress," I said. It was white, with smocking and a tiny bow at the neck.

"This will be much nicer," Dora said, her voice sliding down. "This will be something new, all done by hand, delicate, like lace. I'm sure none of your friends' mothers can make anything like it."

I pulled Silly's dress down over her knees. Her feet stuck out bare.

I looked at the words on the page of the book on the floor. They made no sense.

A frown crossed Dora's forehead, the three lines cutting deep.

"You don't know how pretty it would be," she said, leaving more quickly than she came.

I held on to Silly but I wanted to throw, I wanted to cut.

When Dora got ready to paint the apartment, more stuff got packed away.

She handed me the shopping cart saying wouldn't I like to pull it, smiling a smile that made me not want to. But I was already holding it, and we went up Thorndale and along Broadway to Jim-Ben's Hardware & Paint. The cart made a thwonking sound as the wheels went around. Dora set a quick pace, didn't look in store windows along the way.

Jim-Ben's was old and cluttered, with a dusty front window and a man who'd likely been standing behind the counter for as long as the place had been there. Jim or Ben, I didn't know. Tall and angular, with a grey face and wispy hair to match, and clothes hanging on him.

Along one side were bins with nails and screws, different kinds of plugs, and sandpaper sheets, and above them tubes of glue. On the other side a long row of shelves held cans of paint.

Dora pulled out her list.

"One gallon of oil-based yellow and one quart of white. I'll need turpentine, and two brushes."

She said we'd get a lot of use out of the brushes, with so many rooms, it would be worth it. You had to take care of them, clean them carefully, and make them last.

"What's it for?" the man asked.

"Cabinets, and drawers."

"You know you got to prep it first. You better take sandpaper." He chose some sheets and laid them on the counter along with the brushes and the paint.

"What kind of yellow is this?" Dora asked.

"Yellow, like you said. Yellow's yellow, ma'am."

"There are different shades, of course."

"Not in this kind."

"Turpentine—" He went to get it.

"Your daughter gonna paint too?" He looked at me, chuckling.

Dora seemed startled, and her mouth widened with her eyes.

"I'm sure she can be helpful, can't you, Julia?" she replied. She tried to put her arm around my shoulder.

"Not sure she's crazy about the idea," Jim-Ben observed.

She opened the cart, which took some force, it was bent in so many places. Jim-Ben put in the bag with our purchases. Dora paid and started out of the store, pulling the cart.

It kept squeaking when the wheels went around. It bumped down from the curb as we crossed the street, and Dora frowned.

Dora walked faster and the cart jerked more, and the wheels turned quicker and thwonked more too.

When we got to the back stairs Dora lifted the bag out of the cart. I started to fold the cart to carry it up.

"You can leave that there. It makes such a noise. We'll find something better."

Dora started sanding the cabinets, smoothing out the chipping paint and bubbles and uneven places. To reach the tops of the ones in the pantry she had to stand on the stepladder, which was rickety.

The painting she did while we were at school. The yellow turned out lemony. Dora wasn't pleased, but it was still a big improvement. The outlines and moldings she painted white, together very cheerful she thought, even though the yellow wasn't quite right.

If only she could replace the linoleum, but that would be expensive and we were renting.

For the dining room and Robbie's she brought home color swatches, periwinkle for the one and a darker blue, royal, that's what Robbie would like, for the other. "Sure," Robbie said, shrugging his shoulders. She got a roller and pan and brought them home with the cans of paint in a new shopping cart that didn't squeak.

In the telephone closet she had to plaster first, there were deep gouges where the wall had been clawed beginning long before we lived there. It kept spilling white powder over the chair, the floor, the phone. Each time we went in there we scratched some more. Once it's done, she said, we better stop. Things were going to be nice now.

The hallway was simple, so dark and windowless only white would do. She covered the handprints and ink marks and the faint long smudge where my mother had leaned returning from the bathroom.

Their bedroom, the living room and sunporch were painted in their turn.

Dora began to make curtains, brought home a sewing machine from Sears and showed how cleverly it stitched—lines you couldn't see when you turned the fabric around. She'd teach me how.

For my room she laid out a rainbow of color chips, including special orders they mix before your eyes. We'll make curtains to match.

"Why?"

"Time for a change," Dora said. "Any color you want."

I pointed to a chip of green that matched the catalpa leaves.

"Pink is nice," she said. "And peach." She pointed to a custom swatch. I hated pink, I could imagine what Ginger would say. "It's special-order, it will cost more." She paused and added, "But we can do it," making it sound like a favor.

"Pink's for girls," I said.

"That's right," said Dora.

"I don't want pink," I said.

"This I don't understand." Dora's mouth pushed into a thin tense line. She pushed her hands flat onto the table. Then she picked up the sample sheet.

"Here," she said. She dropped her voice, controlling something, working sugar into it, ending on an up beat. "Here's a green for you." It was pale, almost white, limey.

Okay.

We went to the fabric store and she found a geometric pattern, very modern Dora said, lime and pink triangles and squares on a whitish background. "It's the identical shade," she said.

She was busy getting it ready, then the whole apartment would be done.

My father wouldn't have noticed her improvements, except for the dislocation they caused.

"Very nice," he absentmindedly replied when she pointed out some new addition. And, once restored to his territory, he returned to his papers and his books.

⊗{ 17 }⊗

My father no longer had to come into my room in the morning to make sure I was dressed, or set out my cereal, or open a can for Robbie's and my dinner. When he came home in the evening he sat down to a cold supper with Dora, after we'd had ours. He settled into his armchair behind his newspaper and journals.

He didn't have to sign forms or write notes to our teachers. Sometimes he asked what we were learning in school. He'd tell us more about it.

When I showed my father the world map I'd drawn in school, carefully copying the one in our classroom, "How foolish," he declared.

Miss Kinney had rolled down the map like a window shade from above the blackboard. She drew her pointer across the oceans and continents, tapping the poles, tracing the coastlines of Europe and Africa, the American land mass. We outlined the continents and colored them in.

"Look," my father said, holding up my drawing, "how Greenland is bigger than South America." Surely I must know that was wrong.

For the map in our classroom was in the Mercator projection, so that everything above the equator was huge and everything below the equator was small.

Miss Kinney didn't explain this to us, perhaps she wasn't aware of it, or perhaps she was so used to the map that had hung in front of her classroom for so many years, with which she had taught so many waves of pupils, she no longer noticed or paid it any heed.

The maps in *The World That Was* might not be accurate, but that's because they were made centuries and centuries ago. No one could know then what we know— or should know, my father slyly stressed—now. The world they showed kept changing shape, not just the countries but the continents, the lands and oceans themselves.

A lot of the maps looked more like pictures. Like one with roads and rivers that snaked all over, like Chutes and Ladders. Toy castles sat right side up on one side of the roads and upside down on the other.

Rounded old-style capital letters spelled Syria above, Libya below right, and Gaul—that's France, my father said—below left. Already in the third grade I knew these weren't right. It looked nothing like the map in our classroom.

This was made long before the great explorers, my father explained.

"America," he said, "wasn't even a twinkle in the map-makers' eye."

It was a famous *mappamundi*—a map of the world—created by medieval monks to illustrate the teachings of the church.

"It was the world as they saw it."

Monks were Catholic, like Molly McGwinn, who got out of school early on Wednesday to go to catechism class and told me that I killed Jesus.

Along the edge of the *mappamundi* the monks painted a watery band that surrounds the continents and feeds the rivers and seas. It looks like the rim of a plate.

It's an ancient concept, my father explained—a life-giving body of water encircling the world. The Egyptians and Babylonians carved it in stone.

The ancients feared the water that stretched unfathomable. Its tides swallowed the shoreline and spit it back.

Homer too wrote of a great river, from which both gods and waters sprang. My father uttered Homeric stanzas and quoted from Mesopotamian legends in the German translation he had learned in school.

He read to me about the rivers that watered the arid lands where our distant, distant forebears dwelled. They sustained cities and nourished crops before reaching the sea. Surely there was also a secret place where they began the journey again.

While recounting the legends, my father wanted to be sure I knew the facts—that rivers spring from rains that fall on high mountains and flow over hundreds of miles to the sea. They begin as trickles, rivulets, tiny streams that might disappear in the dry season. As more and more water runs into them, they cut channels in soil and rock and eventually become great waterways, worshiped by the ancients and even today.

Just inside the liquid border of the *mappamundi* sits the Garden of Eden, and out of the Garden several rivers flow. My father said this illustrates what is written in the Bible: that a river waters the Garden, and from the Garden branches into the world. To the medieval monks, the riverine courses out of Eden were real. They believed the rivers flowed under the ocean before emerging to water the world. They plotted the rivers where the Bible described them.

The more you looked at the map, the more things you saw. There was Noah's Ark and a giant layer-cake tower with "Babel" written beside it.

In the Garden of Eden a snake lurked beneath a many-limbed tree. A man and a woman held apples like the ones in the tree. They were naked.

I knew about Adam and Eve, and Noah's Ark, even though I didn't go to Sunday school or catechism like Molly.

The monks thought Eden—Paradise—was on Earth, my father said, that it was on Earth but because of their sin men were forbidden to reach it. On the map this Paradise is shielded by mountains on fire.

These were fables, my father said, which people invented to explain the things they couldn't understand. Primitive people.

"It's an idea of men." Paradise, he meant, which people today call heaven. "An idea of men to make things simpler for them."

"People believe in heaven," I said. They said my mother went there. She was named Eve too.

❧ 18 ❧

By the next summer when I went down the back stairs out the side gate onto Thorndale and around to Magnolia, past the stoop where the mothers sat, I could barely picture her at all. Memories flickered, seeped out of my consciousness. How did I know they were real?

Last summer Leila had sat out there alone watching us, watching in a newly careful way.

Now Dora came out and sat with Leila, and Leila talked to her, the way she had talked to my mother, just the same, or maybe not the same, but close enough, too close. Why was Dora there, watching us? Not Robbie—Robbie was old enough to play in the alley by himself or with his friends. But me and Ginger and the other girls. Mrs. Mc-Gwinn, Molly's mother, wasn't there, she worked.

It was easier to picture my mother on the stoop with the other mothers, talking and watching, than in the apartment, in the sunroom or the kitchen. I couldn't be sure she had been there. I knew she wasn't there still.

The stoop was outside, in front of everyone.

They did not speak of my mother—my father or Leila or the other mothers or Robbie. Robbie just looked daggers at Dora. Robbie slammed his door and didn't come out. Or he went outside and played ball for hours, even by himself, even with no one to play with, instead of doing his homework. I was afraid to slam the door, and I didn't know how to play ball.

The mothers didn't talk about how it had been before.

I didn't think about it jumping rope. You really can't think of anything while you're timing your jump to the rhythm of the ditty and the slap of the rope on the ground. You're singing the rhyme and counting the jumps, jumping double-time and speeding the rope at the end—whether you're jumping by yourself or it's a long rope and other girls are swinging it. It comes so fast, you'd trip if you weren't quick enough. Or roller skating, with the motion carrying you along, free almost from gravity (friction, my father would explain). You had to watch so you didn't catch your skate or lose your balance and fall. The sidewalk didn't slope except at the corners, but the pavement could be uneven. You had to look out for tippy slabs of sidewalk, and you had to slow down at the corner. You could skin your knee, I did it many a time. You don't think about anything. You just feel how fast you're going and try not to fall.

You could get out of breath jumping rope, and roller skating too. You gasp for air when you are done. That's when the thoughts could come—when I was resting, kids were talking and laughing, mothers too. Letting the day cool down, the evening fall before going inside.

The air was mild those afternoons when we played outside and the mothers sat on the stoop, speaking in low confidential tones. I preferred winter, with the bitter winds that sting your skin and produce puffs of condensation out of your mouth. Then there was a reason to feel the burning, the shortness of breath, the knife-sharp cutting of your lungs.

Soon they would stop sitting there. By the next summer we were old enough to play by ourselves. We could cross Thorndale and Magnolia and even Rosedale, the next street over, though not Broadway, only on the way to school, when there was a patrol boy.

❦ 19 ❧

Dora took driving lessons, and one day they brought home a dark-green Chevy. Almost the color I'd wanted for my room, deeper than the washed-out shade it wound up.

Now we could go places.

We drove along Broadway to the Chinese takeout restaurant, waited on plastic-covered chairs, smelled the food cooking, brought home the white paper baskets in a brown paper bag. I chose egg foo yung, which came out of the carton like wet hamburger but inside looked like eggs.

Dora liked to practice her driving along Lake Shore Drive. We came along for the ride, the views of the water, and the fine tall buildings along Lincoln Park. One day we motored all the way to the Science and Industry Museum, where I'd come once with school. I loved going down into the coal mine, and the coal train that took you back in under the earth.

My father had a license from England but he had never driven in the States, so he went out practicing with Dora by his side. He took the road test for his Illinois license. Still, he preferred to let her drive.

On a hot Sunday we piled into the car, rolling down the windows.

"Why can't we go to the beach?" Robbie asked.

"We're going in the other direction," answered my father.

I slid across the seat as far as I could. I set Silly on the left of me, against the door, where Robbie couldn't see her. I clung to the elbow rest.

Robbie asked where we were going, and my father gave the streets and mileage.

"Westlawn," my father told him. "You remember."

"Yeah, but Julia doesn't," I heard Robbie say. "She wasn't there."

I looked out the window.

Dora, in white pants and a yellow shirt with a short white jacket, craned her neck to see over the wheel. She smoothed her pants and touched the controls one by one—gearshift, windshield wipers, turn signals—as if reminding herself where they were. Dora didn't like surprises.

As she turned the key in the ignition Robbie said, "What's she doing here?" low, under his breath. Robbie was looking at the back of Dora's head, where the hair ended at the collar in an even line, so even, it didn't look quite real. His hands clutched white around his baseball cards.

My father turned around and looked at Robbie and at me—that's who he thought Robbie meant—and said, "I told you not to say 'she.'"

We headed out on Lawrence, my father reading the map. We drove west till the buildings thinned out, fields came in between, patches of corn. As the car went faster, the wind blew strong into the back seat. It pushed hard against my face, sent my hair straight back.

I felt carsick in the back seat. I leaned against the door, feeling Silly at my side.

At a crossroads we came to a stop sign, two roads meeting like pickup sticks that land in a perfect X. The corn was cut back from the corner, then it started again.

"Pulaski," my father said. "Turn left."

The road stretched flat and straight ahead of us. The cornfields raced alongside. When the car went slow you could see the leafy hands reaching up and the tassels on top, but when we went fast they passed like a tall, green blur.

Then the corn dropped away and the land was empty again. Fields of dirt appeared with small boxy houses, some of them still being built. At Montrose, Dora turned again.

"We need flowers," she said.

"There's a florist along this road," my father told her. He unfolded the map. "Just past Austin, on the right." He looked up, read the street signs that were starting to appear, checked the map. "It should be soon.

"Slow down," he told her.

Buildings were coming closer together.

"There." My father pointed to a fruit stand sitting in front of a greenhouse. Dora pulled into the gravel drive and stopped the car.

"Wait here," my father said as the two of them got out.

Robbie followed them with his eyes. He pulled some baseball cards out of his pocket and started shuffling through them, holding them so I couldn't see the faces. He read them out: "'Hank Sauer, thirty-seven homers, a hundred twenty-one RBIs.' How about that! 'Ralph Kiner, thirty-seven homers.' 'Robin Roberts, twenty-eight and seven.'"

"You didn't give the homers."

"He's a pitcher, dummy."

I tried to get a look at the cards, but he pulled farther to his side of the car. I stroked Silly's hair. It was ratty and in clumps now. Her dress was dirty. Dora wanted to wash it.

My father came out with a cone of green paper, stems sticking out of the narrow end. He held the flowers away from himself, telling Dora to open the trunk. They were dripping, did we have any newspaper to put down?

My father opened the map again, as Dora started the car. "Now we must watch out," he said, in a different, sudden voice. "We're almost there."

A high iron fence came up on the left.

"This is it," said my father. Dora slowed the car and turned in between two tall stone pillars with plaques that read "Westlawn" on one side and "Cemetery" on the other.

Inside the drive forked. Grass stretched over small rises and under spindly trees in a thin pale carpet, not deep green like Lincoln Park.

My father pointed and Dora followed the right-hand turn, steered slowly around curves. Metal plaques on thin posts appeared with the names of flowers. "Lily." "Marigold." "Dahlia."

Dora went around another curve, seemed to go back the way we had come. I could see the corner of the fence and across the road some of those new houses without any trees.

"Perhaps we passed it," my father said. "What's that sign up ahead?"

"'Carnation,'" Dora read as she slowed the car.

It was "Rose," just past "Carnation."

"'Rose,' of course," my father said as Dora pulled the car to the side.

My father and Dora got out of the car, and he pointed across the grass. Robbie opened his door and slid out.

I held Silly against my chest. "We'll wait here," I said.

I kicked my foot against the front seat. We're safe here, I told Silly, pulling her closer. This isn't for us, remember?

"Come out now," my father said.

I kicked my other foot. I put both arms around Silly. My father looked into the car.

"See what marks you've made on the seat," he said. "Get out."

I braced my feet against the seat back and pushed, wedging myself hard as I could. I put my right hand down, trying to hold onto the seat.

He reached in and grabbed my arm. My legs lost their hold. I felt myself slide, Silly slipping out of my arm. I stuck my legs out again. My father had to pull hard, jerking, to pry me loose. I kicked my feet whichever way I could, hit air, the hard car door, my father's leg. He yanked me with a big sudden force, stood me against the car. His hand went up and came down before I could close my eyes, but it missed, or changed its mind, did not make contact.

He slammed the car door.

Dora was holding the flowers which she'd taken out of the trunk.

My father marched off, Dora alongside. Robbie and I followed. My father traced between the headstones, glancing down, looking but hardly slowing.

They split and each covered an area, one left and one right. The stones were more scattered here, the rows only partial. Dora was the one who found it.

"Let's put the flowers down," my father said, and Dora started to unwrap them.

There were flowers there already, a patch of little purple blossoms growing up to the stone. Dora put down some of the new flowers beside them.

"You made a good choice," my father told her. "They are lovely."

Lovely, mouthed Robbie.

"Come, put some flowers down," said Dora. She handed a few stalks to Robbie, who barely touched them and, making a face, dropped them onto the stone.

My father leaned down and moved them to the side.

"Your turn, Julia," Dora said, holding three flowers out in front of me.

I wrapped my arms around my stomach, felt something lurch inside me. I couldn't help reading the stone before I had to look away.

I was going to be sick. All I could do was spit—spit it out, just small droplets of spit out of my mouth.

My father saw and grabbed me and opened his hand,

let it make contact this time.

The sick came all the way up now, out of the taste in my mouth.

They made me take off my dress for the ride home, stuck it in newspaper in the trunk. Dora pulled out a jacket of hers and put it around my shoulders.

"I don't want it," I said.

"You have to."

"Hey, Dad," Robbie started when we got into the car, "Sauer hit two yesterday. That's fourteen."

"At that rate," my father said, "how many will he have at the end of the season?"

"I dunno. How should I know?"

"You can figure it out."

"How? I don't know how many."

"How much of the season has been played?"

"I don't know," Robbie said, shrugging.

"You've learned proportions," my father said. "You did it last year."

"Last year he hit thirty-seven."

"Last year in school! Now think, how many games are over, and how many left to play."

"How should I know?"

"Approximately. We don't have the newspaper here, so you have to estimate."

Robbie looked out the window, curled his upper lip, and let the cards slide through his fingers.

❦ 20 ❧

When Robbie was studying world history but didn't want to be, my father brought home a box with a globe and put it in on the dining room table and called Robbie and said, "Here, this is the world." My brother loved the globe on the *SS America* when we came over, my father told him, a huge globe in a floor stand in the wood-paneled library. "You twirled and twirled it." Robbie didn't remember.

"Look," my father said. "Here are Spain and Portugal, where the explorers sailed from." This is what they were studying in the sixth grade.

My father didn't often bring us things. My brother nodded but wouldn't look. This wasn't what he wanted from my father.

"How will he learn anything?" Dora said, coming out of the kitchen. Robbie saw her coming and got up and went into his room.

Robbie would rather play baseball in the alley with Joey than study the explorers, or anything. Robbie spent hours throwing and catching in the alley, and batting if there were enough boys. My father watched some of the Cubs games now that we had a television set, and sometimes we went to Wrigley Field. But it wasn't something you did instead of homework.

Every day when Robbie came home from school Dora would tell him he better start his homework, his father would be home before he knew it. The more she said it, the less Robbie listened, and the quicker he headed outside. Actually Dora said "Daddy," as if it was the most natural thing in the world for her to say.

Joey would play anytime, he didn't care if he did his homework. The nuns at St. Regina's cared, he said, and they'd rap him on the hand if he talked back, but not if he dreamt up some excuse. They cared more about how neat the homework was than what was in it. He couldn't be neat even if he tried, Joey said, so he didn't try. Sometimes he talked back to Sister Michael because she didn't hit kids. Lots of the nuns had men's names, Joey said. The boys dared each other to see what they could get away with, and sometimes Joey got sent to the principal's office. He didn't get away with it then.

On Sunday Joey's father sometimes came out and played ball with him in the alley, tossing the baseball back and forth or pitching so Joey could practice his hitting. If Robbie was out there, he'd give Robbie a turn, and Joey would play the outfield. My father never played ball even on the weekends. He sat in his armchair studying his books. He told Robbie you have to study if you want to learn anything.

Our principal didn't rap your hand with a ruler the way the nuns did. I didn't get sent to the principal's office. But she sent notes home about Robbie to my father. Sometimes my father boxed our ears. I didn't know if it was better or worse than the ruler. He'd say, "I'm going to box your ears," and sometimes if you stopped whatever it was, he didn't, but sometimes once he said it, it was too late anyway.

Sometimes Robbie would say things under his breath that he thought my father couldn't hear, or maybe he wanted him to hear but wanted to be able to deny it. Like at the dinner table when Dora asked Robbie whether he had done his homework or when was he going to get back from the movies or playing ball, which Robbie didn't think she had a right to ask. My father could be off with his own thoughts and notice things with his other eye, or ear. "Look at your mother when you're spoken to," he would say, as if out of the blue. Robbie mouthed *mother*, curling his lip.

I didn't talk back like Robbie. Sometimes I couldn't get the words out at all. I would open my mouth as if getting ready to speak, but then it was all I could do to breathe.

Joey didn't go to the summer day camp at the Lutheran church kitty-corner from our building, but Molly did, even though she was Catholic. Charlotte went too. Charlotte said they were Baptist but they didn't go to church, only to summer camp. Robbie and I didn't go anywhere, not to church of course or Sunday school or camp.

Sometimes if Joey or anyone wasn't around Robbie picked up an old tennis racket my father had given him, which was heavy and beat-up, and went to hit a tennis ball against the wall of the Kroger's across the alley. He'd come in when it was time for dinner.

Robbie was getting pretty good at tennis and once in a while my father took him to play at some weedy cement courts on the other side of Clark Street. Robbie had a natural swing but he didn't run enough, my father said. They played a set, and my father chased down every ball. Robbie got close but he couldn't win. My father didn't let him win.

"Steering is the key," my father told me as he gripped the saddle of my new bicycle. I pedaled shakily along the sidewalk. I held my breath, lost my breath, not from exertion but fear.

Molly McGwinn was looking out the window of her apartment, across Thorndale. Molly already knew how to ride a bicycle, though she didn't have one.

Robbie was playing baseball in the alley with Douglas and Joey. Robbie had a bike, he was almost four years older than me. "You're not riding my bike," he said that morning as I untied the bow on the present. They couldn't wrap it, it was too big. "Even if you learn how."

The pavement was coarse and pebbly. On the right was the rough red brick of our apartment building, on the left a strip of grass and then the curb with cars parked.

I pedaled as fast as I could, trying not to look at the sidewalk. My father quickened his step.

"Steering, Julia," my father said. "Steering is the secret."

"I'm steering," I said. "I'm trying to go straight."

I tried to get air into my lungs.

"If you turn the handlebars too far, you'll fall over," he said, trotting beside the bike, still holding on. "But if you don't steer, you'll fall too." He chuckled.

The catalpas hadn't leafed yet. They had puffy green clusters all over them and tiny petals drifting down.

"Look ahead." my father said. "Keep moving."

I held the handlebars firm, pushed one foot, then the other, looked down, jerked and started to wobble. My father had let go of the seat. He grabbed it again. I slowed, I put my feet down.

The bike was blue, with wide chrome fenders, rubbery black handlebars, and "Schwinn" written in swirly letters on the shaft.

"If you don't go fast enough, the bike will fall down," my father said. "You have to keep going.

"It's a marvelous invention, the bicycle," he said. "A great feat of engineering. The best ideas are simple."

He had brought out the encyclopedia to show how a bicycle works. How the rider has to keep steering and pedaling and the center of gravity keeps you in balance. How the first bicycles were funny old things, with one huge and one tiny wheel, and the rider pedaled directly, there was no chain, it was much harder.

My father couldn't, or wouldn't, change a light bulb, but he could tell you how the light worked.

"Put your foot on the pedal, and then the other one, and then go," he said.

"I'm holding it," he said. I pedaled, he walked. "Faster," he said. I pedaled faster. He let go. I could feel myself in the air, the bicycle going. I saw the alley up ahead. I slowed, it wobbled. I felt dizzy and put my foot down.

"The bike has to reach a speed," my father explained, "where its momentum carries it forward. Otherwise it will fall."

⌘{ 21 }⌘

My father wanted us to know how the world works, by the laws of physics.

He described the arc of a baseball thrown from the mound and its resulting speed and direction once it made contact with the bat, why it went right or left, flew over the centerfield fence onto Waveland Avenue or into the glove of the left fielder.

He explained how the play-by-play came through radio waves, pulsing long and short, transmitted through towers, beamed out, received by the antenna, sifted by the tuner to get the station Robbie dialed to.

He taught us how to count after the lightning flash until we heard the thunder. Now divide by five. Now time the next one. Is it bearing down or racing away?

He took pages from yesterday's Chicago *Tribune* and folded up boats and floated them in the bathtub. First he made a square, then a diamond, then he folded the edge over to make a hat. Then he turned the hat inside out. If we blew hard the boat scudded to the other end of the tub, just like the wind pushing a sailboat across the lake.

Wind is caused by differing air pressure, my father said. The molecules rush in to where the pressure is low. Water displacement is why the boat doesn't sink.

So much of what we know about the world, how it looks and how it works, my father liked to tell us, the Greeks figured out millennia ago. They observed the sun and the stars, recorded the tides, used the sundial and the astrolabe to calculate distances and angles. Pythagoras— of geometry fame, as I would learn in high school—declared that the earth was a sphere, Eratosthenes figured out the size of the sphere, and Aristarchus concluded that it went around the sun. Eratosthenes mapped the world as the Greeks knew it. In the big blue atlas, it looked a little like a crab, with the Mediterranean between its claws, the Northern Ocean flowing across the top and the Atlantic along the bottom.

My father applauded the logic of the Greeks, their keen powers of observation, and, most of all, their persistence in applying the scientific method to what they found. We would do well to follow their example. It was the basis of science, of his work, of—he hoped—my education.

My father measured for me the spaces between the planets, when I was in the seventh grade, my science project to illustrate the theories of the origin of the solar system, with papier-mache balls stuck onto wires suspended from holes punched in a cardboard box collected at the supermarket. I molded the balls in different sizes, as best I could, and laid them out on the table according to their order and placement. I lined the inside of the box with dark-blue paper, splashed some dots of white as stars, and painted the balls a lighter blue before sticking them onto the wires.

There were limitations to our model. The distances—Uranus and Neptune nearly forty times as far from each other as Venus is from Earth—became lost in translation to the scale that had to fit our box. The inner globes we placed close together, the farther ones we spaced out. Those were the only distinctions we could make. The sizes, too, were relative; I could not build Jupiter hundreds of times bigger than Earth. This bothered me, oddly, more than him. After all our work, I wanted our model to be precise, but it represented the solar system only in the crudest way. My father, though, was satisfied with our handiwork. Hanging on their dark, almost invisible wires, the wads of blue paper looked nearly like planets in space.

❧ 22 ❧

We moved closer to the hospital and bought another car for my father to drive to work. In our new house he had his own study, a separate room, where although he didn't close the door—he liked to call out for things and be heard—we knew to stay out. The papers and books piled up once again, islands growing on his desk and on the floor around it, barrier beaches protecting the far shore.

My father still brought out his atlases to fill in my blanks. He made sure I could find the Greek city-states. He wanted me to grasp the breadth of the Holy Roman Empire at its peak.

He'd compare the centuries-old maps in *The World That Was* with the *Hammond World Atlas*, acquired to help with our homework. He quizzed me on the changing empires, the shifting boundaries.

We revisited the *Holy Land Atlas* and borrowed *Exploring the Bible: Myth or History?* from the library. We learned that in our own time, against all odds, archaeologists have searched for the Garden of Eden. One followed a route described in cuneiform tablets, over craggy mountains to a lush valley dense with fruit-laden trees. Another using topographic maps placed Eden at the ancient confluence of the Tigris and Euphrates, just above the Persian Gulf.

Some think Eden was in Eridu, in Mesopotamia, right next to Ur, whence our patriarch Abraham came. Eridu had its own sacred garden. Long before the Bible, Eridu's god punished man for eating the fruit of a forbidden tree. In Sumerian, "edin" means "plain."

My father weighed the merits of their various theories. We located their landmarks on Hammond's Middle East spread.

We moved even though Dora had redone the apartment, but that was a few years back, and it was still an apartment with linoleum on the kitchen floor and wooden back stairs covered in grey paint.

We traveled by car through quiet streets lined with the elms that were still around then and oaks that supplied carpets of acorns and notched brown leaves. We raked them into a wire basket and my father lit the match, sending up sweetly fragrant, now-forbidden smoke.

My school was modern, all on one floor, with low ceilings and metal-framed windows that opened sideways. The floor was soft tile, like linoleum, muffling the hallway sounds.

They assigned a girl to take me around, Maritsa, a strange foreign name, but she wasn't foreign. She had smooth black hair that curled just under the ears and a self-assured voice, like a teacher's. All the kids seemed older, especially Maritsa.

Here they had different teachers for different classes and we went from room to room all through the day.

Maritsa thought I must have come from a backward place, with only one teacher, always the same kids together. She wanted to know about my friends and thought Ginger a strange name for a girl, she'd had a cat named Ginger, a marmalade cat. Ginger's hair was dark, I said, almost like Maritsa's, though not as stylish, not stylish at all, which I didn't say.

We had science in a lab with shelves holding chemical bottles and equipment, and tables with sinks to do experiments. The subject in eighth grade was Earth science, something we hadn't heard of at my old school. On the globe decorating our textbook, *Our Earth,* clouds whirled above the continents and seas. This wasn't yet a satellite image taken from space but still only an idea of what it might look like.

We studied how the earth formed and why it looks the way it does—earthquakes and volcanoes and floods. We learned about the upheavals that created the Rockies and the Andes and the Himalayas, growing taller even as we spoke.

Our teacher, Mr. Belden, wore longish hair, rimless glasses, and a mustache before these were in style. He carried a novel, not *Our Earth*, into class. He diagramed the earth's cross-section in colored chalk on the blackboard, from crust to mantle to core.

He told us all the continents had eons ago fit together and had ever since been drifting apart. He outlined on the board a supercontinent he called Pangaea and challenged us to find the forms we knew. He clued us in that they'd been squashed together, hadn't looked exactly as they do now.

The way the continents drifted apart, with their huddled shapes and shifting coastlines, reminded me of the maps in my father's atlas. From the bulky, conjoined Pangaea, the continents spread, grew distinct, became recognizable. From one corner of the globe they scattered to the places they hold today.

They're continuing very, very slowly to move. Not that we need to worry—we won't notice for millions more years.

We wouldn't find Pangaea ("all the earth" in Greek) in our textbook. It was a concept put forward by a German scientist named Alfred Wegener to explain the fact that the coastlines of South America and Africa matched perfectly, with rocks and fossils that corresponded remarkably too.

Wegener was born, like my grandfather Friedrich, in Berlin in 1880 and, like Friedrich, developed his ideas while recuperating from wartime wounds. In *The Origin of Continents and Oceans,* he contended that the continents themselves move around on the denser mantle. Where they slide apart they widen the oceans, and they build up mountains where they collide.

Although, or because, Wegener drew on many disciplines, geologists ridiculed his revolutionary ideas. Only later did evidence build to support his theory, which finally, as our teacher predicted, would become mainstream.

My father saluted Mr. Belden for teaching us about Pangaea. Finally I was learning something worthwhile.

But the American history we studied he thought was small potatoes, and the westward expansion, which we mapped with colored pencils, not worthy of our time.

He'd pull out the *Schul-Atlas* and, turning the yellowed pages, show me how people had always been on the move. We followed them: Alexander the Great and Hannibal, the Visigoths and Vandals, the Tatars and the Ottoman Turks. Out of the Fertile Crescent they came, across the mountains of Europe, the steppes of Russia, wave after wave, expanding, shifting, the outline changing from one map to the next. Nomads and searchers, armies crossing whole continents and more. Amazing migrations over thousands of miles, on foot, on horseback, on camel, soldiers carrying swords and women with babies wrapped against their backs, cooking pots and bedding too. How did they know where they were going?

And when they arrived, did they discover they had left something behind, something irretrievable? Was the earth too black, or too sandy, the trees too towering, with oddly shaped leaves, and birds singing a strange song? Perhaps they no longer knew where they had come from, perhaps only their parents or grandparents had been there. Did they still carry some image that would never again be seen, some yearning that would never be fulfilled?

◈{ 23 }◈

After school Maritsa would come over and we sat in the kitchen, Dora at the counter on a high stool, Maritsa and I at the table part, a little lower, on regular chairs.

I noticed how Dora's hair was almost as smooth as Maritsa's, and glossy, not wiry like mine. Dora cut my hair like hers and said how alike we looked, but it wasn't the same hair. They resembled each other, Dora and Maritsa, thin and athletic, trim. Maritsa moved languidly, Dora briskly, but they shared an economy of motion. Nothing extra, nothing unnecessary.

Maritsa with her exotic name had never met anyone with an accent before.

"Your mother's different," she said later, meaning it as a compliment.

Maritsa started hanging around listening to Dora's opinions and trying to get Robbie's attention. Robbie had tried out for baseball and said the reason he only made junior varsity was he was new in the school, they didn't know him. He was going to decide whether it was worth it to play. He was checking it out.

Robbie had gotten tall but not as tall as he wanted to be. He still shot baskets over the closet door with a tennis ball, doing a play-by-play. Our next-door neighbors had a hoop over their driveway, but Robbie seemed to prefer his own game.

He paid little attention to me now, only to comment occasionally on my figure, thick around the middle, or on my boring, sickeningly boring good grades. Who was I cozying up to now?

He wasn't going to notice Maritsa either. She was only in the eighth grade.

When we moved it was easier not to have to tell the whole story, letting the picture stand, the way it looked. When Dora went to register me for school, no one asked, they assumed she was my mother. She certainly didn't correct them.

I didn't correct Maritsa either. The long-ago images had slipped away, clouded over.

What had happened I was no longer sure of, knew only as a fact, a piece of data, as if it had happened to someone else. Maybe I would report it, casually, to Maritsa, and maybe I wouldn't.

I had not been such a small child, too young for memory. But if it is true that all our cells replace themselves every seven years, perhaps mine simply gave out. The new ones had no memory of what had gone before.

In my new room, with windows on two sides and fresh white curtains, when I looked in the mirror there was only my own face, so imperfect, vague and disconnected. It wasn't a face I recognized from anywhere, from anyone. My clothes were the sensible ones Dora picked out, meant to be slimming—"This will suit you"—beiges and browns, not to call attention, A-lines, pleated pants.

I could only measure myself against what I was not. I had lost the picture of what I was, where I came from.

Had it been a charmed life? Had it been blessed? Had it been?

"I can't tell if you look like her," Maritsa said.

"Who?"

"Your mother."

I didn't say anything. Maritsa looked at herself in the mirror, looked at me, back and forth.

"Do you think you do?"

"I don't know," I said.

V

Rivers of Paradise

❦ 24 ❧

My mother left, not with another man, and not all at once, but little by little, pieces of her falling away. She didn't pack suitcases, she didn't make arrangements, she didn't bring back a present.

She slid out of reach, over that place where the earth curves, where our ancestors believed it ended. They needed to be careful.

Now we know better: The horizon is continuous, the earth is round.

"We," perhaps, but not I. She fell off this edge. It is out there, I know.

Things went blank, whole continents froze up and covered over and disappeared. Where were the footprints, the markers?

The landscape was laid waste, the maps redrawn.

I no longer knew where we had started, what it had been like to have her. A spirit fled, like ghosts, like gods no longer believed in. I carried on like one of my grandfather's patients, missing a limb.

I dig, trying to discover what I had, what I lost. I listen for the music that must be somewhere, like the light of stars so far away we see their deaths a million years later.

I splice together fragments like the crumbled pieces of an ancient scroll, put back together by scholars believing: This is where we must have come from.

I have been a diligent pupil, studying maps, gathering data, piecing together fragments to make a picture of the world.

Nowadays people set off for Morocco, to bargain in the souks of Fez and follow Berber guides high into the Atlas Mountains. They explore the pyramids of Mexico, the temples of Cambodia, the megaliths of Easter Island, astounded by the particularity and commonality of the human endeavor. They hike through the remotest valleys and up the sharpest of peaks, declaring their wonder.

I, instead, seek answers on charts and maps, in books and on paper. I am looking for evidence, a sign, a proof which is not in the world.

The world is too complex, you can only see what is in your field of vision. What happened long ago has vanished from the landscape you walk through. If it left footprints, they have been washed away.

The *Schul-Atlas* shows caliphates and khanates, the trade routes of the Vikings and the Genoese. The globe beside my desk plots the routes of Columbus and Magellan and Captain Cook. You will search for them in vain on the steppe or in the forests or the oceans. You cannot find them in the world.

I don't aspire to climb Mt. Kilimanjaro, with its lush trails and thin air, as so many do today, when the world is so small, as they say, and they have already trekked across

Nepal, not to mention the Alps. In the atlas I can discover that Kilimanjaro rises nineteen thousand feet above the Masai Steppe, in Tanzania, near the Kenyan border.

I love the way mountains look on a map, yellow shading into pink and then brown, so that they seem to actually rise up from the paper. On the wrinkly contours of a topographic chart, the kind you can order from the Geologic Survey, concentric circles climb the hilltops. Narrowing furrows mark the slopes. You can almost place your foot on the very hillside. It is a perfect description, it is more exact than the mountain itself.

On a topographic map of Chicago you won't see any contours that define a valley or a hill. The few faint lines wander lazily parallel to the lake. In our old neighborhood there isn't a single one.

You can find our streets on the gas-station maps my father collected, even before we had a car. He taught us how to read them. The maps unfolded like cutouts and quickly split in the corners and along the seams. We had to be careful not to tear them completely apart. My father never threw a map away, even when he got a new one. He penciled the date on the top.

The road map shows the north-south, east-west grid of the level, spread-out, unornamented city. There are Thorndale and Magnolia and the next streets over, Elmdale and Ardmore. These are the blocks we traveled, the pavements where we played and skated. Beyond Elmdale lies Granville and, still farther, Devon, where we went to double-feature Saturday matinees at the ornate, cavernous Granada Theater.

Along the straight Chicago streets stretched low buildings like the deli across Thorndale and the drugstore on Broadway, owned by our downstairs neighbors, almost celebrities for that. At the corner of Winthrop loomed my school, with the swings, much bigger than Ginger's, attached with great steel links, and the ice rink when they flooded the playground in winter. We left our shoes in the puddly fieldhouse, skated round and round in the short light and the grey cold that I never minded.

On Broadway, which I crossed every day on the way to school and back, stood the patrol boy and the Kroger's that backed up to our alley. In one direction was Charlotte's house and the Chinese take out, and in the other Jim-Ben's Hardware, where Dora led me pulling my mother's shopping cart. A dusty, disorganized shop, perhaps because Jim and Ben didn't want people looking through their things, they wanted to do it themselves. This was back before the days of self-service. There is a hardware store in my town like that today, the walls lined with little drawers holding nails and screws and bolts, shelves with cleaning supplies, and little bins with electrical outlets, switches, cords, and plugs.

The shopping cart had squeaked so, the wheels crooked and hitting one of the cross pieces. Dora pulled it home loaded with the paints and turpentine and brushes. I left it at the bottom of the stairs.

Dora had come to take care of us, to set things straight. I should have been able to stop it, but I couldn't.

❧ 25 ❧

I would have become a mapmaker if I could draw, if I could hold a pen or brush and limn a line that's firm and clear and wavy only where it's meant to be wavy, not because I can't hold the pen properly. I'd hold the pen tightly but not too tightly, a pen of the kind you don't see any more these days, with a proper nib, wide at the bottom. It's a special skill, using a pen like that.

I would trace the continents first, a clear solid outline, shading a little on one side, using the thicker part of the pen. I'd use a finer point to fill in the boundaries, the roads and the railways. I would picture in my mind towns with tile roofs on sharply sloping hillsides, as I imagined the people in the houses that raced past the window of the Denver Zephyr when I was six years old, and every train I have ridden since then. Maybe I would sketch in the bridges, the monuments. I might give the waters a special flourish, like the cartographers of old, with striations along the flowing rivers and gentle waves on the circling sea.

The mapmaker decides what is and was and even might have been, what will be recorded and what passed over. He paints cities and empires unseen for millennia, fortresses and figures that maybe never were. He imparts his vision and his truth.

With pen and paintbrush, on parchment and in fresco, mapmakers have depicted the world they knew, or imagined. Potentates and slaves, camels and palm trees populate the lands. Jumping fish, spouting whales, and many-masted ships ride the oceans. Around the edge, from every direction, wind-heads blow.

In their beloved Holy Land, mapmakers rendered concrete and incontrovertible the mysteries of Scripture. On a battlefield David slays Goliath and on a mountain-top Moses, in blazing light, receives the tablets of the law. In the Garden of Eden grow pale green trees on short straight trunks, and Adam and Eve stand eating the apple, a minuscule snake at their feet. In a decorative insert, an angel with upraised sword pursues them.

In Genesis, in the medieval *mappamundi*, the rivers flow down from the Garden, where mortals cannot go.

The waters of the Garden are pure and fragrant, and the trees bear fruit and flowers year-round.

But the waters once they enter the world, the monks believed, have lost their sweetness. There is an aftertaste, minerals, grains of limestone and granite washed from the rocks, soil carried by rain and floods. You cannot taste the nectar of the ever-ripe fruit or the honey petals of the ever-flowering blossoms. You may drink and drink and you only imagine these tastes. They have not washed down to our world.

You might follow the river upstream searching for the fountain from which it springs. It flows under the ocean or the land, you are cut off by the flames or the unscalable peaks. You cannot get there.

If only we can trace the waters, we will find the Garden again.

Perhaps they flow down a hillside, through a valley, and, lazily, over a plain. Perhaps they cut through a forest, beneath tall, dense trees. Beside the water there may be a path, narrow and cushioned by pine needles, barely visible through the greenery.

If I were a venturer, a believer, a barefoot child, I would enter the forest. With the trust of a seeker, farther and farther into the woods I would go. I would follow the path alongside a stream.

Deep in the forest perhaps I would meet a shaman, his face deeply lined but his eyes bright, the last of a tribe of priests who once dwelled in the woods.

With incantations the shaman awakens the spirits. Across the great divide he travels, at great risk, to call them forth.

He defies the boundary decreed by monks and rabbis and physicians—the line between the quick and the dead.

He restores what has been lost.

The shaman sees wounds that are invisible. The pain remains, but of what is it a reminder?

The people bring him their afflictions and their secrets, their desires and their losses. Even what may have vanished long, long ago, even what may have been forgotten. Even people today, in our world, who, against all reason, believe in magic.

Were I one of them, I could see the shaman with my own eyes.

To the shaman, the waters are pure. They may come from Eden, but they are not adulterated, nor condemned by sin.

With a gourd the shaman would scoop water from the stream and let it wash over me.

The water would caress my skin, the mist graze my limbs. I would remember the hot sand and the icy waters of Lake Michigan, and how when I came out of the water shivering, my mother threw a beach towel around me, and warmed me, and held me close.

❦ 26 ❧

Today I return to the dense green canopy of catalpas sheltering Magnolia Avenue.

The catalpa is a strange, humble, untidy tree, with its oversized leaves and bean-like fruit that ripens and falls. Catalpas grow quickly, like weeds, and live a long time. They don't grow straight tall trunks and shapely crowns like the oaks and maples that grace boulevards and parklands and farmsteads. A catalpa sends out crooked branches hung thickly with odd, fluttering leaves.

Catalpa leaves are notchless and stubby and can grow almost a foot across, and the long, dark, ripply pods look like they fell from Mars.

But the ragged, verdant catalpas of Magnolia Avenue create a surprising and wondrous shade. It is not dark, like a close-packed forest, or impenetrable, like a jungle. It is not like one of those Midwestern streets where the tall, stately oaks meet midway across, high above houses set back on wide lawns. It is rather space entirely filled, from the street above your head to the tops of the buildings— mostly three-story, six-flat apartments like ours—with an airy, diaphanous, deep-green shade.

It is beneath the jagged-barked, big-leaved catalpas that the mothers sat, on the stoop in front of our building. It is here that I last saw her, where I can place her, when other memories and pictures—confiscated, supplanted, corrupted by double-exposure—cloud over. Here in her house dress and ankle-strap sandals.

The catalpas mark the center, the point of the tiny radius of that childhood world—just a block in one direction, a few more in the other. At its farthest, the limits are Bryn Mawr and Granville, Sheridan and Clark. Anything beyond is foreign and unreachable.

The catalpas make a world, the streets mark its boundaries, as the trees and rivers of Mesopotamia mark the location of Eden.

The map of Chicago does not show the catalpas and their high, miraculous shade, or the stoop, or the figures beneath the trees.

The map does not reveal the people on the way to the Kroger's with the slow-moving cart, as the maps in my father's atlas showed the figures in the Garden of Eden, and the track of Abraham's journey. You cannot see the mothers on the stoop or the girl roller skating, or playing Simon Says, or coming up the back stairs, home from school. Or jumping rope as fast as she can, gasping for breath, not knowing why, and unable to speak as she follows along Broadway from Jim-Ben's and abandons the shopping cart in the yard.

If I were a mapmaker I would draw the catalpas, but I could not show the figures beneath them. They would be hidden. Catalpas grow in disorderly profusion, not neatly like the arbors of Paradise. From the sky, from heaven, from the bird's-eye view of the eagle or the migratory tern on its way to South America, you cannot see clearly. The trees are too dense.

As I sit on the stoop on a warm, humid summer day, a river of moisture wafts on the breeze. It caresses my arms.

It grazes my face. Like a shaman's blessing, it restores.

The fragrant heat takes me back. The mother and the daughter return to me—not exactly seen but believed.

Maybe the catalpas of Magnolia Avenue, like the map-makers' trees in the desert of Mesopotamia, are the only evidence I will find.

The trees grow miraculously in the Garden of Eden. The rivers nourish the God-given trees. Gracefully the rivers join and branch—scarce waters in an arid land.

The waters once they enter the world are no longer perfect. They pick up sediment as they cut through canyons and flood plains, and grow steadily cloudier along their course to the sea. Still, you dip your gourd into the stream in quest of their sweetness—the blessing of the waters that flow from the Garden, the Garden of our forebears, of our eternal, irretrievable past.